Death and the Visiting Fellow

By the same author

Fiction

Unbecoming Habits
Blue Blood Will Out
Deadline
Let Sleeping Dogs Die
Just Desserts
Murder at Moose Jaw
Caroline R
Masterstroke
Class Distinctions
Red Herrings
Brought to Book
The Rigby File (ed)
Business Unusual
A Classic English Crime (ed)
A Classic Christmas Crime (ed)

Non-fiction

It's a Dog's Life
John Steed – the Authorised Biography
HRH The Man Who Would Be King (with Mayo Mohs)
Networks (Who we know and how we use them)
The Character of Cricket
The Newest London Spy (ed)
By Appointment – 150 years of the Royal Warrant and its Holders
My Lord's (ed)
The Duke – a Portrait of Prince Philip
Honourable Estates – the English and their country houses
A Life of Love – the Biography of Barbara Cartland
Denis – the Authorised Biography of the Incomparable Compton
Brian Johnston – the Authorised Biography
Beating Retreat – Hong Kong Under the Last Governor
A Peerage for Trade – a History of the Royal Warrant
Village Cricket

Death and the Visiting Fellow

Tim Heald

ROBERT HALE · LONDON

First published in Great Britain 2004

ISBN 0 7090 7578 2

Robert Hale Limited
Clerkenwell House
Clerkenwell Green
London EC1R 0HT

2 4 6 8 10 9 7 5 3 1

Typeset in 12/15pt Times New Roman
by Derek Doyle & Associates in Liverpool.
Printed in Great Britain by
St Edmundsbury Press Ltd, Bury St Edmunds, Suffolk.
Bound by Woolnough Bookbinding Ltd.

This book was concieved when I was myself a Visiting Fellow at an Australian University. I would like therefore to dedicate it to my friends, colleagues and former pupils at Jane Franklin Hall in the University of Tasmania and at the University of South Australia in Adelaide. Absolutely no resemblance to any of these wonderful people is intended – nor indeed to my equally wonderful all-Australian wife, Penelope, whom I would also like to include in this dedication.

CHAPTER ONE

Death and the Visiting Fellow arrived almost simultaneously.

Or so it seemed.

Doctor Tudor Cornwall, Reader in Criminal Affairs at the University of Wessex, collected his bag from the airport carousel shortly after 0800 hours on 1 October, carried it through the green channel, signifying 'Nothing to Declare,' and emerged blinking into the reception area where he stopped. In front of him there was the usual crowd of uniformed chauffeurs, tour company reps, apprehensive relations and black market cab drivers. He gazed around, searching for the familiar figure of his friend and host, Professor Ashley Carpenter. There was no sign of him and Dr Cornwall frowned.

He and Ashley had spoken shortly before his departure from England. Ashley had wished him 'bon voyage' (some hope, travelling for over twenty four hours in economy) and said he'd meet him at the airport. Tudor had said there was absolutely no need and he'd get a cab up to the college and see him there, but Ashley had told him not to be ridiculous. He was always up at six to take the dog for a jog. It was no big deal to motor the half hour to Hobart International. They could stop off at the Egg'n'Bacon Diner on the way back into town, have a heart attack on a plate and catch up on the news. They hadn't seen each other since the Toronto conference. That was nine months ago.

The two men had known each other since Oxford many years before. In those days Ashley was the dashing Rhodes Scholar from New Coburg – a muscular oarsman who stroked the college eight and could have had a Blue for the asking were it not for the long hours in the lab where he was already establishing a reputation as a whizz in the world of forensic pathology. Tudor was reading history and developing a fascination with crime down the ages which was to define his career and make him almost as distinguished in his branch of criminal activity as Ashley in his. Tudor's interests were catholic, ranging from 'Who killed Perkin Warbeck?' to 'The incidence of rape in the little wars of Queen Victoria'.

In the normal course of events their paths would never have crossed. Unlike Ashley, Tudor was a 'dry bob'. His sports were racket-based with a particular bias towards the obscure but historically interesting game of Real Tennis. (Frederick, Prince of Wales, was killed by a Real Tennis ball in circumstances which Tudor found deliciously intriguing though eternally baffling.) Their work took them to different destinations. The historian was always in the college library, the Radcliffe Camera or Bodley itself. Ashley was always elsewhere, cutting up corpses, staring at X-rays, specimens and samples. Ashley's friends tended to be other Australians and New Zealanders; Tudor mixed with friends who, like him, had been to traditional, if minor, English public schools.

It was a girl who brought them together. Both of them pursued Miranda who was a great beauty, famous for her Juliet in the eponymous Shakespearean play, for her eccentric cloaks and striped trousers, for her wit, her charm, her everything. Like half the university, Ashley and Tudor courted her and though for a time they both had more success than most (she actually accepted invitations to dinners that neither man could properly afford) their rivalry ended in rejection and despair. Yet there was a silver lining to this melancholy affair. The two men found themselves ruefully comparing notes, then consoling each other, and before very long finding that they enjoyed each other's company and had quite forgotten Miranda – who eventually succumbed to a dim philosopher from Trinity. Tudor and Ashley had been friends ever since.

Memories of those early days passed almost subliminally through Tudor's brain as he scanned the crowd at the airport concourse. Definitely no Ashley. It was not like him. He was normally fastidiously neat and punctual in all that he did. Almost obsessively so. Tudor put down his case and ran a hand through tousled salt and pepper hair. More salt than pepper these days.

'Doctor Cornwall?'

He looked down from his considerable height and saw a small tubby fellow in a lumberjack shirt and coffee moleskins. The man seemed agitated though relieved to have made contact.

'They told me you'd be tall,' he said, 'and you seemed the tallest fellow around. I'm Davey. Brad Davey.' He put up a hand which Tudor took and shook hardly realizing what he was doing. 'I'm Executive Assistant to the Principal,' said Davey. 'She said she was sorry not to come himself but she's sort of tied up. The police. They're asking questions.'

'What's happened?' asked Tudor. He realized that he was shaking and had broken out in a cold sweat. Intuition as well as his life's work told him to expect the worst. 'Is Professor Carpenter . . . I mean is Professor Carpenter all right?'

Brad Davey looked embarrassed.

'We don't know,' he said. 'It doesn't look too good. They found the car but there's no sign of the professor. He seems to have vanished. Could be all right. But it's not like him. The police say they're treating it as suspicious.'

'Oh do they?'

Doctor Cornwell picked up his bag.

'I'm sure there's a perfectly rational explanation,' he said, 'There nearly always is.'

CHAPTER TWO

Tudor had never been to Tasmania before and he knew little about it beyond what Ashley had told him. Ashley talked lyrically about Tasmanian 'life-style' but at the same time acknowledged a need to 'get off the island' at least every six months. Hence his addiction to academic conferences.

'Far away place of which I know nothing,' mused Tudor, as he and little Brad loaded his cases into the back of a battered shooting brake. The Visiting Fellow was travelling light as was his wont, both physically and metaphorically. He hadn't gathered a lot of moss in life so far. Others, especially women, accused him of 'lacking commitment'. Tudor shrugged and pretended not to understand what they meant. Privately he thought they might have a point.

He straightened up and gazed around. Brad had parked the car immediately under a 'No Parking' sign just outside the 'Passenger Arrival' entrance. The airport was single-runway, single-terminal, middle-of-nowhere-much. Tudor found himself looking up at steep mountains covered in thick foliage dotted with grey outcrops of granite. In places the trees seemed to have lost their leaves so that they dotted the hillside like phalanxes of poles, not natural at all.

'Bush fires,' said Brad, following his stare. 'Scary, but I guess they're nature's way of spring cleaning.'

There was further evidence of bush fire on the road to the city. Some of the remains of the trees were charred black, others were a silvery white, almost luminous.There were few houses at first and most of those looked like little more than log cabins. The land seemed barren and scrubby. The road, dual carriage, not busy, skirted the occasional lake and sea inlet. Presently the number of houses began to increase until they were passing suburbs – row upon row of neat bungalows each with a garage and an identical plot of lawn about a third of an acre in size.

'You get a great view of Hobart just round the next bend,' said Brad, 'Not quite Oxford's dreaming spires or downtown Manhattan but we sort of like it.'

Tudor caught the mixture of pride and defensiveness he had met before in off-shore islanders.

'You from Tasmania?' he asked.

'Born and bred,' said Brad. 'Been here all my life apart from a year travelling. This is home. And look, there she is . . .' He pulled the car over on to the hard shoulder, turned off the ignition and leaned forward, arms crossed atop the steering wheel. Below them, a mile or so away, lay the little city. At its heart there was a prickle of utilitarian high-rise blocks. Fanning out from this downtown area, the roads were lined with much lower buildings, mostly red-roofed. There was a lot of green too: parks, gardens, tree-lined avenues. Apart from the hard core of concrete and glass, Hobart was a garden city. Between the shooting-brake and the waterfront was a wide estuary spanned by a single low-slung bridge. Behind it, lowering over the entire cityscape, was a single dominant mountain.

'Mount Wellington. I call it the Wurlitzer,' said Brad, 'mainly because of that organ-pipe formation you see all along the rim of the summit, just above the tree-line.'

'I see,' said Tudor. 'They *do* look like organ pipes. Wurlitzer's a much better name.'

'They found the car up there,' said Brad, 'Professor Carpenter's. He must have gone for a walk.' He giggled nervously. 'Keen walker, Professor Carpenter. Good too. Knows what he's doing. So if he has gone walkabout there's no cause for concern. He can look after himself. Mind you, just because the Wurlitzer's so close to the city, doesn't mean to say it isn't wild up there. The other side's wilderness for two or three hundred miles. Nothing but bush. Thick. No features. Odd he didn't tell anyone what his plans were, especially with you coming. He was looking forward to your visit.'

Brad shook his head, took off the hand-brake, engaged first gear and eased the vehicle back on to the highway. Tudor found himself not much liking Brad Davey though he would have been pressed to explain quite why. There was something mildly if indefinably creepy about him.

They did not speak again until they had crossed the bridge over the Derwent River and passed into the city itself. Then Brad pointed out the sights and sites in a terse tour-guide manner. Tudor nodded in perfunctory acknowledgement, managing little more in verbal communication than the occasional, 'Mmmm.' It occurred to him that something of his gut-dislike might have got through.

'I'm sorry,' he said. 'It's been a long flight. And I'm concerned about Ashley.'

'Sure,' said Brad. 'No worries.'

Huh, thought Tudor, worries are exactly what we have. But he said nothing and they drove on in silence until five minutes or so on the other side of the city, in an affluent inner suburb in the foothills of the Wurlitzer, they turned left down a drive bright with spring rhododendrons, and drew up outside a handsome nineteenth-century mansion built in warm ochre sandstone. All around it, stretching back and flanking well-maintained lawns and flower-beds were more modern blocks.They had a 1960s custom-built appearance.

'Welcome to St Petroc's,' said Brad. 'You're in the Old Building. Top Flat. No elevator but great views and you've even got a little roof terrace. Neat.'

Tudor had no very clear idea of what to expect but was pleased when they climbed to the third floor. The apartment had a large living-room with views to the river and mountains beyond, all the usual facilities and, perhaps best of all, a spiral staircase which led up to a railed patio with table, chairs and pot and even better views.

'Dame Edith,' said Brad, 'would like it if you could join her for lunch. Very simple. Just the two of you. In the lodgings. Twelve-thirtyish.'

'Where exactly are the lodgings?' asked Tudor, mildly amused by the archaic Oxbridge word.

'Downstairs,' said Brad. 'The front door leads off the hallway. There's a brass plaque and a bell. It's really just a garden flat but Dame Edith is a stickler for traditional usage. You'll see this evening. It's a High Table night. If you didn't bring a gown you'll find one in your cupboard. We meet for sherry in the Senior Common Room at six. Jacket and tie.' He pulled a face. 'The further you get from the Mother Country the more like the Mother Country we behave.'

The Visiting Fellow laughed. 'I can't remember the last time I wore a gown,' he said, 'We're very informal at Wessex. Very shirtsleeve order.'

'Well,' said the principal's assistant, 'that's not the style at St Petroc's. We like to do things according to the book. Now I have to dash. I have a tutorial coming up. Do you have everything you need? If you want to take a look round you'll find the students really helpful. There's a college bus every half-hour which runs down town and then on to the main campus. Doesn't take long. Just explain you're the Visiting Fellow.'

'I think I'll just unwind, unpack, maybe have a bath and forty winks,' said Tudor. 'I'm a bit knackered to be honest. By the way, can I use my lap-top for e-mail?'

'Sure. No problem. There's a phone jack. Just dial '9' for an outside line.'

'Great.' He gave an unenthusiastic smile.

'My extension's 208 if you need me. The college office is 200. The girls there will help you all they can. We're here to make you feel at home. I'll see you at High Table.'

Tudor exhaled deeply as the door closed and he was left on his own. He sat down on the sofa, wondered whether to smoke a calming cheroot but thought better of it. His body clock said it was around ten in the evening rather than mid-morning but that was too bad. The sooner he *tried* to acclimatize, the sooner he would actually do it. He ruled out a medicinal duty-free brandy on the same grounds.

The sofa was soporifically yielding. He kicked off his shoes, put his feet up and relaxed. The prospect of Dame Edith Arthur was intimidating. She had a formidable reputation even though running St Petroc's was, by her standards, a twilight job. She had been Federal Minister of Culture in her prime and, subsequently, a popular High Commissioner in London. Her immense study of the Echidna or *Tachyglossus Aculeatus* was the definitive work on that curious antipodean cousin of the hedgehog and the porcupine. Dame Edith had a reputation for being as prickly as the animal on which she was the world's leading expert: unmarried, outspoken, erudite, elderly but unbowed.

Tudor walked to the window and examined the view. A chunky tramp steamer was chugging up the Derwent like something out of Masefield. The city was laid out below him like a map. Apart from the modest array of modern blocks there were several church towers and a lot of green. 'Ships, towers. temples and domes,' he murmured, and unbuckled his largest case. Unlike most men he was a fastidious packer. His clothing was clean and neatly folded. Carefully and methodically he conveyed them to drawers, hooks and hangers. He had brought with him his three core books – a *Concise Oxford Dictionary*, the *Oxford Book of English Verse* – the first edition, edited by 'Q' – and Julian Symons' majestic survey of the crime novel, *Murder Bloody Murder*. Bedside reading was, in his experience, best locally acquired, but without these three volumes he felt intellectually crippled. He was a reasonably competent user of the Internet but he had not yet found any electronic substitute for certain books. He liked the feel of paper between his fingers and too much screen-watching gave him a migraine.

Nevertheless, his laptop had become almost as indispensable as *Murder* and the two Oxfords. The Tasmanian telephone socket was not the same as the British one so he had had to invest in an expensive kit from some specialist in computer bits and bobs. To plug into a Tasmanian server he first had to convert to the American system and then onward to an Australian one which, of course, was the same as Tasmania's. Too tiresome. He opened the bag and stared blankly at the cat's cradle of wires and sockets and sprockets, then decided to have a bath before attempting to establish a connection with e-world.

He dozed off in the warm water but woke before it became uncomfortably cold, then shaved, dressed in clean clothes, and, feeling refreshed and dapper, dealt with the electronics in no time at all. He had one message waiting, transferred it to his in-basket, disconnected and pressed 'Get'.

The message was short, reassuring and yet perplexing.

Welcome, it said, *to Tasmania. Sorry not able to greet you in person.See you soon, but meanwhile stay stumm and don't tell anyone I've been in touch. As ever, A.*

Tudor Cornwall stared long and hard at the screen, then shook his head and looked at his watch. Almost time for lunch with Dame Edith. He turned back to the computer and frowned for a moment before pressing the delete button and watching the words disappear from view.

'Anything you say, Ashley,' he muttered, 'but I wish you

wouldn’t play silly buggers. Especially when I’m still practically in mid-air.’

Saying which, he switched off, adjusted his tie and cudgelled his mind in search of something to say about the echidna.

CHAPTER THREE

Dame Edith looked like Mrs Tiggywinkle, an anthropomorphic coincidence which could not logically have had anything to do with her lifelong obsession with the echidna but was still curious enough to raise Tudor Cornwall's extravagant eyebrows. She was short and round and dressed in various shapeless garments ranging in colour from beige to tobacco brown.

'Ah Dr Cornwall,' she said, appraising him over half-moon spectacles as he walked towards her apprehensively across a threadbare carpet.Her room was a clutter of books and papers from floor to ceiling. Crossing from her door to her desk was an obstacle course as Tudor slalomed gingerly between piles of texts and tomes.

Her handshake was firm and her gaze steady.

'Sherry?' she enquired. 'I think you'll be amused by its presumption. It's Tasmanian. A splendid little winery up in the hills near Padstow. Wallaby Creek. Charming family called Mendoza who came out from Seville in the eighteen nineties. The grandfather made guitars for Segovia. Full without being fruity and just a hint of hazelnut. Or I have loganberry juice if you'd prefer something non-alcoholic.'

Tudor smiled.

'Thank you. A glass of Wallaby Creek would be very nice.'

It was too. He sipped as he was bidden and sat as he was told in an elderly leather chair out of which most of the stuffing appeared to have been knocked. The chair was large and clubbish and it was only when he had sat down that he realized that it already contained a large ginger cat. The cat, not quite squashed, raised its head and bared its teeth reproachfully, if a little light-heartedly.

'Don't mind Fergus,' said Dame Edith. 'He's perfectly friendly unless roused.'

Tudor smiled. He was not crazy about cats but they seemed to like him. Sure enough, Fergus stretched, arched his back, and moved, with supreme confidence, on to Tudor's lap, where he lay purring. Tudor used his spare hand to stroke the cat's head without enthusiasm.

'You should be flattered,' said the Dame. 'He doesn't usually like strangers.'

Tudor said nothing.

'I'm sorry,' said the Dame, after a lengthy and slightly awkward pause, 'that your friend, Professor Carpenter, wasn't here to greet you.'

'Likewise,' he said.

'I'm very fond of Ashley,' she said.

He saw no reason to doubt her.

'So am I,' he said. 'We go back a long way.'

'So I understand.' She sipped her sherry and looked at him speculatively. A difficult debate appeared to be taking place inside her head. Eventually it seemed that a vote was taken and the matter resolved.

'I'm afraid there may be a problem with Ashley,' she said.

Tudor said nothing but looked quizzical. The cat purred. On the mantelpiece a handsome, though tarnished, carriage clock whirred briefly and struck the quarter. Outside an ill-tuned car changed gear with much grating. Student car, student driver, thought the Visiting Fellow. In their day he and Ashley had ridden bicycles. Only a very few of the rich and privileged had owned cars. He remembered an obnoxious army lieutenant on full military pay who drove a scarlet MGB.

'It's complicated,' said the Dame, 'and absolutely nothing has been proved. So I hope I can rely on your discretion.'

He nodded.

'We have a thief in the college,' she said. 'It's not uncommon in communities such as this. But it's tiresome. For a number of reasons I prefer to solve such problems without recourse to outside help. Quite apart from anything else it sends the right signal to our students. They have to learn self-sufficiency. Besides, with a resident expert such as Professor Carpenter, it seems really rather superfluous to ring in the local constabulary. Why hire a mini-cab when there's a Rolls-Royce in your garage?'

Tudor smiled.

'I'd say Ashley was more of a Ferrari than a Rolls.'

Dame Edith glanced at him sharply.

'Many a true word . . .' she said. 'We had our suspicions almost from the first. It was nothing dramatic. Petty cash mainly. No matter how much you lecture people on the need for security they persist in leaving their rooms unlocked and they will leave banknotes lying around, wallets on desks, credit cards with PIN numbers written in diaries. Sheer carelessness, but they're children. They don't understand. They always think it can't happen to them. In this case the culprit is obviously a young woman I've had my eye on for some time.'

'How did you come to suspect this particular girl?'

Dame Edith sighed. 'I blame myself,' she said. 'She was a borderline case from an academic point of view, but she was severely disadvantaged socially. A lot of alcohol at home, poverty, possibly sexual abuse. I felt sorry for her. And she'd worked hard against the odds. I felt she should have a chance. We gave her a scholarship but our funds are limited and there was only so much we could do.'

She sighed and sipped, then continued.

'She did some waitressing to help out financially. Then I heard she was working in a bar with a very unsavoury reputation. I confronted her with it and she denied even knowing the place. I think, to be honest, that she became frightened. Then, suddenly, the thefts started. We'd had nothing of the kind for at least two years.'

'What made you think it was this particular girl?'

The Dame smiled. 'Motive first,' she said, 'though I have to concede she wasn't the only student with money worries. Character second. I don't mean that she was a wicked girl, but she was . . . is . . . weak, easily tempted. Opportunity third. She wasn't very sophisticated about it. Most of the people who reported things missing were in the same building as her.'

'All circumstantial stuff?' asked Tudor rhetorically.

She nodded.

'But,' he continued, 'you had your suspicions even though you knew they were based on intuition?'

'That's another reason I wasn't keen to call in the police. I had a hunch, well, it was more than a hunch to be honest, but I had no proof.' She grimaced. 'And if it was Elizabeth I really didn't want to think in terms of a prosecution. A criminal record would be a disaster for her. She's on a knife edge in any case.'

'So you asked Ashley to investigate?'

'It seemed sensible,' she said. 'He did some clever things with fingerprint powder and a hidden camera. Don't ask me. I'm a zoologist not a policewoman. Within a couple of days he had conclusive proof. But unfortunately he made a mistake.'

The Visiting Fellow frowned. 'Ashley made a mistake?'

Tudor Cornwall was surprised. His old friend was not a mistake-maker.

'Oh no,' she laughed, causing Fergus to raise his head. 'Nothing to do with his forensic procedures. He was profession-ally as immaculate as we'd both expect. No, he made a different sort of error. He confronted the girl directly and without a witness. He asked her to his room after dinner.' She shook her head. 'Silly boy!' she said. 'Silly, silly boy!'

There was a knock on the door and the Principal said, 'Come in.' The door opened and an Indian in a maroon blazer and matching turban entered behind a trolley loaded with sandwiches, fruit, a jug of water, plates, cutlery and glasses.

'Thank you, Sammy,' said Dame Edith. 'And, Sammy, this is Dr Cornwall from England. He's our Visiting Fellow this semester.'

The Sikh bowed seriously at Tudor who smiled back, before looking enquiringly at his boss and being told that he had done all that was required and they would serve themselves. When he had closed the door behind him, the Dame said, 'He's got a proper name but he complained that we all pronounced it wrong and it's so long since we tried that none of us can remember what it was. He's been 'Sammy' for as long as I've known him. He came as a gardener but he's been college butler for the last five years. He knows everything about everything at St Petroc's. And then some more.'

'Did he know about your college thief?'

'I should imagine so. I wouldn't dream of asking him though. He'd think it frightfully bad form.'

She rose to inspect the sandwiches. 'Smoked trevally, local beef with horseradish and Whale Island Blue cheese,' she said. 'The college bakes its own bread. Do help yourself.

'So the inevitable happened. Elizabeth refused to admit anything and then came to me the following morning to complain that she'd been sexually harassed by Professor Carpenter.'

Tudor almost choked on his smoked fish. He had never tasted trevally before and just as he was in the act of swallowing his first mouthful he was confronted with this ludicrous suggestion.

'For heaven's sake,' he said. 'When it comes to sex, the one thing Ashley does not need to do is to start groping students.'

'I know that,' she said, chomping on bread and cheese, 'and

you know that. Others may not. It's the girl's word against his. But there's worse. She's not stupid. She was back twenty-four hours later with the president of the junior common room and signed depositions from three other girls, all alleging that they had been sexually molested, propositioned, harassed or interfered with by your friend . . . and mine, Professor Ashley Carpenter.'

'So when was all this?'

'The day before yesterday.'

They ate in silence. Tudor was not happy. He thought briefly of telling the Dame about the e-mail message he had picked up earlier in the morning, but he discarded the idea as soon as he contemplated it. It was important to play his cards close, not reveal his hand, wait for others to show theirs. He had no idea who held the trumps. His only possible ace card was the knowledge that Ashley was alive and well and sending e-mails. But even that was supposition not certain fact. Anyone could have sent an e-mail in Ashley's name. It wasn't like snail-mail. You didn't have handwriting to identify. You didn't even need to know Ashley's ID or password. Tudor was only semi-literate when it came to computers. He used his laptop just as he used his car. He could drive it well enough to get from A to B. If it went wrong he rang the AA or took it in to the garage. He supposed that he could send Ashley a message and ask some clever question to which only Ashley would know the answer. But even though that might prove that Ashley was alive, it wouldn't prove anything else. The professor could have been kidnapped. He might be being held against his will, sending e-mail answers with a knife at his throat or a pistol at his head.

'This smoked fish is delicious,' he said. 'So what's the plan?'

'Plan?' The Dame seemed not to understand his question.

'What do you intend doing?' he asked.

'Doing?'

Tudor found this second repetition irritating.

'Well, with respect, you're potentially on the brink of a serious and potentially embarrassing situation. Petty theft is one thing; you could probably hush that up without too much of a problem. Sexual harassment is something else again. It's all the vogue. It could lead to a huge amount of unwelcome publicity for Ashley, St Petroc's, you, even for Tasmania. People write books about this kind of thing.'

'Quite,' said the Dame, picking up another sandwich. 'That's why I'm relying on you.' She smiled, almost wolfishly. 'In fact, I think you're my only hope. Ashley's told me lots about you and I've read quite a lot of your stuff on organized crime in pre-industrial society. And your Robin Hood book of course.'

Tudor groaned inwardly. *Robin Hood – the Crook the People Crowned* was his first and still most popular book. He hated being reminded of it.

'Well,' he said, and embarked on a suitably self-deprecating life history. He didn't enjoy it but he didn't really see any alternative. He could have killed his old friend Ashley.

Always assuming he wasn't dead already.

CHAPTER FOUR

After lunch, Tudor took a walk. He needed to clear his sinuses. The combination of cat and Tasmanian sherry coming so soon after the stale, recycled, germ-ridden air of his flight from Europe had played havoc with his tubes. He craved fresh air. Also, like a jockey before a race, he liked to walk the turf before competition was joined in earnest.

It was shortly after two by the time he came down from his eyrie and stepped out into the garden quad. It was a pity about the buildings, he thought. The 60s had a lot to answer for when it came to architecture. St Petroc's had the utilitarian cardboard-box feel of a thousand and one utilitarian cheap brick concrete and plate glass blocks in Tasmania's mother country. On the other hand, someone had laid out a pleasant garden and spring was springing. The 'old' building itself was overlaid with a profuse pale purple wistaria. Trees blossomed. They looked like cherries, though horticulture was not Dr Cornwall's forte.

As he emerged from the building which was not only the heart of the college but also the only edifice of anything approaching distinction, he noticed an atractive blonde in baggy white shorts, a skimpy blue top and a New York Yankees baseball cap. She was sitting alone at a wooden picnic table staring at an open foolscap folder and sucking on the end of a pencil. As Tudor came out she glanced up and flashed him a broad smile.

Hi!' she said. 'Can I help?'

'Er . . . hello,' he said. It was not exactly a 'come hither' smile. Under cross examination he could not honestly say that it was more than just friendly. It was not the girl's fault that she was attractive. Her T-shirt was very tight and she was not wearing a bra. Tudor found her nipples disconcerting. She was lightly tanned, had even white teeth and dimples. Tudor had an uneasy feeling that she had been waiting for him.

'You must be the new Visiting Fellow,' she said.

'Well, yes, actually, but how do you know?'

'Well,' she said, laughing, 'you're a strange face, you're coming out of the old building, and you're a Pom. So you just have to be the Visiting Fellow. Anyway, hi, I'm Elizabeth Burney.'

She held out a hand and he shook it, alarm bells ringing. The look she gave him clearly conveyed some kind of complicity though, once more, he would have had trouble convincing an unprejudiced third party that it went in any way beyond simple friendliness.

'Also you look lost,' she said. 'Would you like me to show you round?'

Tudor considered. He was uneasy but he was tempted. After all, why not? He wanted to find his sea legs, and the girl obviously had local knowledge.

'That would be very kind,' he said.

She stood. Good legs, too, Tudor noticed, then realized that she was young enough to be his daughter.

'It takes twenty minutes to walk down town,' she said. 'You like to see down town?'

He was intending to walk there anyway. He had intended to do so on his own and unattended. He was happy with his own company and tended to learn more when solitary. On the other hand, it would seem churlish to turn her down.

'By the way,' she said, 'I'm supposed to be the college thief.'

She smiled again. 'Not true, of course. But it's a long story. Maybe if I get to know you better I'll tell you about it.'

Tudor had heard that Tasmanians were famous for being open, frank and forthright, but this was ridiculous. He wasn't at all sure how to respond. The English part of his character told him to retreat behind his English veneer of *sang froid* and stiff-upper-lippery. His natural middle-aged caution urged restraint, but something else told him not to be so bloody pompous, he was in Tasmania now so stop being so impossibly buttoned up. Let it all hang out. And, no, it had absolutely nothing whatever to do with sex. He was far too grown up for that sort of thing. Besides the girl was far too young. Also her appeal was too obvious, too 'in-your-face'. No, no, the polite thing was to accept gracefully: he might learn something. After all, Dame Edith had asked him to help her out. How better than to interview this prime suspect.

'Downtown,' he said, fatuously. 'That would be very nice. Thank you.'

'Great,' she said. 'I'll just put my Gallipoli notes back in my room and I'll be with you. Thirty seconds.'

She was as good as her word and a minute or so later the two of them were striding purposefully in the direction of downtown Hobart.

'Is this your first time in Tasmania?' she wanted to know, though she barely waited for the answer before volunteering the information that she had always wanted to visit the UK and see where her ancestors came from. The original Tasmanian Burney had been convicted of some form of petty theft and transported there for the term of his natural life. He had stolen a sheep, she thought, or possibly a lump of coal. Doctor Cornwall was tempted to ask if larceny ran in the family, but he thought better of it. Not, judging by her performance so far, that the girl would have minded. But you could never be sure and it was not Tudor's style to take that sort of risk.

He wondered also whether it would be politic to raise the matter of his friend Ashley and the girl's charge of sexual harassment. However, that too seemed better left for the moment. Cowardice, politeness, common sense? He thought it was a little bit of all three but he was forced to acknowledge that he was prejudiced.

Outside the college they turned left down a leafy avenue of large sandstone mansions. Gardens were bright with lilac and laburnum; drives were blocked by Volvos and BMWs. Through kitchen windows, colonial pine dressers could be seen, cluttered with blue and white china and tall glass jars containing preserved fruits and vegetables. This was Cuisinart country where Condé Nast magazines shared coffee tables with the *Wall Street Journal* and the *Investor's Chronicle*. Every city in the developed world had districts such as this, just as they had no-go slum ghettos. The inner suburbs of the rich all had their cultural peculiarities, but whether it was Dublin or Durban, Moscow or Melbourne, Newcastle or New Orleans their similarities were greater than their differences. Their inhabitants would have been entirely at ease at each other's dinner parties, tennis clubs, bistros, delis, car boot sales and weekly worship. The dads watched CNN, the kids wore Nike or Adidas trainers and mums co-operated on the same school run. Which brought one back, inexorably, to the Volvo and the BMW.

At the end of this stockbrokerish Arcadia, there was a main road where the houses either cowered behind high walls,or had been taken over by professional businesses of the sort that advertised themselves with brass plates: orthodontists, chiropractors, real estate developers, attorneys-at-law, colonic irrigators. All had interminable letters after their names – FRSCol.Irrig. (Saskatchewan) and suchlike, though nothing quite as sad as the BA Hons (Oxon Failed) which Dr Cornwall had read about but never seen.

Some houses, wooden-slatted with rusty wrought-iron

balconies, looked as if they were in private hands but on the whole they were ill-kempt and looked as if they provided cheap, rented accommodation. There was little evidence of house-pride. Occasionally a shop occurred and these were consistent with the arterial quality of the highway. Instead of the bijou, upmarket, expensive, one-off emporia of the salubrious oases to either side of the highway, these were chain convenience stores – drive-through off-licences, snack bars offering meat pies, pasties and deep-fried chicken drumsticks.

All this was at one and the same time quintessentially Tasmanian and peculiar to Hobart, yet also familiar. Perhaps even depressingly so. Doctor Cornwall felt he had not come to the far end of the earth in order to be confronted with canned Guinness and massed produced Pizza Margarita. If he had wanted a Big Mac he would have stayed on campus at the University of Wessex.

'I guess you have McDonald's in England,' said Ms Burney.

'I'm afraid so.'

'I know what you mean.' She wrinkled her nose. 'Where I come from in the north of the state you still get old-fashioned steak sandwiches. You know, with the lot. Old-fashioned white bread, and thick, brown gravy, half a pound of sirloin, fried egg, tomatoes, onion, cucumber, mayonnaise, pineapple, ketchup, mustard, lettuce, beetroot.'

'Goodness,' said Tudor, aware that he was sounding prissy. 'All that in a single sandwich.'

She looked at him with amusement and scorn. 'You poms!' she said. 'You don't know what a sandwich is. Slicely thinned cucumber and the crusts cut off. Call that a sandwich? Get out of here!'

Tudor grinned. He was beginning to quite like the college thief.

'Where are we?' he asked. 'Where are we going?'

'This is the main road in to the city from Pippin Valley,' she said. 'Standard drag. In a minute or two we'll hit the Isle of Wight Barracks; then the Real Tennis Court and Dettingen Look Out. Then it's real downtown: Gucci, Pucci, Davidoff, Ripitoff. Made in New York, made in Rome, Paris, London, Tokyo, Hobart. Know what I mean?'

She laughed. And Tudor found himself liking her even more. Part of him was saying 'Help!' and the other part, 'Lucky me!'

They walked on in silence. Outside the gates of the Isle of Wight Barracks were two vintage twenty-five pounders and a small cenotaph in memory of the dead of the two world wars. A sentry in khaki shorts stood in a box. He was wearing a bush hat and carrying a stubby black automatic which looked too modern for the rest of him. A hundred yards further on, Tudor saw what he thought was a pub sign swinging gently in the breeze. It consisted of two antiquated-looking gold tennis rackets on a black background. Underneath the rackets was the date 1873.

'Real Tennis?' he enquired, looking up at a sandstone barn of a building with windows just below roof level. It was set back from the road with a neat lawn in front of it.

The girl nodded. 'Some Pom governor brought it out. It's weird.'

'I know,' said Tudor. 'I used to play it once a long time ago. In fact it was when I was at university myself. Actually I used to play with Professor Carpenter.'

She glanced at him sharply but said nothing.

'Perhaps I should take it up again,' he mused, half to himself.

'Do you want to check Dettingen Look Out?' she asked. 'It's the nicest part of Hobart.'

'What is it?'

'It's the old area round the look-out. Beautiful old warehouses and there's this fabulous tower right at the end by the harbour. They used to have a man up there twenty-four hours a day keeping watch for ships. They stopped that but anyone can climb up. It has three hundred and sixty five steps. One for every day of the year. Great view from the top but it's steep.'

'I'll save the climb for another time,' he said, 'but I'd like to have a look.'

So they turned right off the main road and soon came on a wide cobbled avenue flanked by fine warehouses, the ground floors of which had been converted into health-food shops and wine bars, ethnic clothing stores and all the arty-crafty outlets associated with the *mildly* trendy, *almost* alternative life-style Tudor had seen in similar developments elsewhere.

'There's a fabulous market here every weekend,' said the girl. 'Not just food and drink. There's fortune-tellers and jugglers and a fire-eater. You know, street theatre.'

Tudor nodded. He had seen lots of that sort of market in his time.

They walked on to the water's edge where the tower stood. There was a stone set in the base with an inscription which said that it had been laid there by His Grace the Duke of Dorset, Commander-in-Chief of British Forces in Tasmania 1803. The structure was imposing – a colonial campanile soaring high into the southern sky.

'It used to be a favourite spot for suicides,' said the girl, 'but they put reinforced glass round the viewing platform. Nowadays most people jump off the harbour bridge.'

She shaded her eyes and gazed up at the column. 'Way to go,' she said.

Rusty fishing boats lined the quayside, several of them selling their catch of the day. Scales and fins gleamed in the sunlight: purplish squid, silver salmon, ebony eels. Away to the left, one of the warehouses had sprouted a glassed-in terrace overlooking the water. It was a seafood restaurant called Roddy's. Outside the door there was a picture of a voluptuous mermaid wearing a chef's hat. Cornwall looked up at the sky and shivered slightly though not from the cold.

'Well, yes,' he said. He wondered again if he should broach the subject of the girl's sexual harassment charge against his old friend, but again decided against it. He needed to do some thinking.

'You've been very kind, Elizabeth,' he said. 'I've taken up much too much of your time. Very selfish of me. Thanks very much for guiding me here. It would have taken me ages to find it for myself. But you must have lots to be getting on with.'

She took the hint with a swift assurance which surprised him.

'My pleasure,' she said. 'Can you find your way back to the college?'

'Oh, I think so,' he said. 'If not I can always take a cab.'

'Sure,' she said. 'See you around. In fact I'll see you this evening in Hall. It's a formal dinner night.'

'Yes, of course,' he said.

She gave him a wide flirty smile and walked away through the crowds with long extravagantly coltish strides. Tudor Cornwall watched her go, smiling after her, and felt a strange sinking feeling.

CHAPTER FIVE

Cornwall dressed for dinner.

As he did so he mused. Part of his musing was devoted to Hobart itself. This, after all, and despite impending excitements, was to be his home town for a semester. (Semester was not a word he liked, but it appeared to be part of the St Petroc's vocabulary and when in Rome . . .) What he had seen of Hobart seemed agreeable in a mildly old-fashioned, genteel sort of a way. It reminded him of Bournemouth, only further away. Perfectly congenial for a couple of months though he suspected that anything a lot longer might have seemed uncomfortably like a prison sentence. He couldn't help remembering that part at least of the colony's original purpose was penal. The present-day city, however, seemed blissfully innocent and unthreatening. He knew such appearances could be misleading. What was it Holmes said to Watson? 'Not all the vilest alleys of the city can produce more horrifying crimes than this smiling and beautiful countryide.'

Quite so.

He also found himself musing on the girl with no bra but dismissed these thoughts as inappropriate and potentially dangerous for a Fellow of the College, even a merely visiting one.

And finally, of course, he mused on the whereabouts of his missing friend. This was a puzzle and his musings were therefore inconclusive and frustrating. It was not like Ashley to shirk confrontation.This, more than anything, was what bothered him. Mystery was second nature to him. And Ashley also liked playing games. If he had simply disappeared and said, 'Come on, find me!' Tudor would not have been particularly surprised. Irritated maybe, but he would have thought it more or less in character. 'Oh, Ashley's up to his old tricks.' But on this occasion it sounded as if his friend had a problem. True, his e-mail message sounded breezy and cheerful enough, but that was easily fixed. No, all his experience of Ashley told him that he was a man who always faced the music. If he had done a bunk it was not because he was under threat even of sexual harassment. The charge was the one which modern academics feared more than any other, but even if there was any substance in it – and Tudor was certain there wasn't – Ashley would never run away.

Even so, the thief with no bra was disturbingly fanciable.

Dinner was not a black tie occasion but Dame Edith had made it plain, in the nicest possible way, that a jacket and tie were *de rigueur*. So was an academic gown. Such formality was far from the norm at the University of Wessex which tended to be laid back and informal in most matters, particularly sartorial.

This place almost took Tudor back to the days of his youth before scruffiness, *laissez-faire* and egalitarianism. Jack was now as good as his master and the student as his teacher. Although it was politically incorrect to admit it, Tudor found this tiresome and unfair. In his undergraduate days he had definitely not been allowed to think himself in any way the equal of his tutor. Indeed, his tutor had been allowed to talk the most fearful tosh without fear of contradiction and Tudor had looked forward to the time when he would be allowed to do the same. This had not happened and it made him peevish. Now that he was in his prime he had to listen to his students talking almost as much rot as his teachers a generation or so earlier. And political correctness decreed that he was not allowed to contradict them. No justice. Not much sense either.

He decided on his dark pin-stripe with a plain blue silk tie just wide and vivid enough to hint at something marginally less staid than the rest of his exterior suggested. First impressions were so important. He glared at himself in the mirror, bared his teeth, slapped his cheeks, tightened the tie, smoothed the hair and winced. A few months earlier an anonymous reviewer in *The Wyvern*, the University of Wessex's student magazine, had described his lectures as 'elegant, amiable and undemanding'. The faint damn rankled. He could be *extremely* demanding.

High Table convened in the senior common room for pre-prandial sherry. Doctor Cornwall was one of the last to arrive. He was late-ish but not exactly late so the gathering was almost safely gathered in. Conversation was hovering somewhere between hum and hubbub on the vocal equivalent of the Richter or Beaufort scales: noisier than just polite but quieter than quite convivial. Dame Edith was standing in front of a leather-topped club fender warming her ample bottom in the glow of a pungently fumed log fire. It smelt of juniper.

As Tudor entered, she beamed in his direction and made a beckoning gesture with her sherry glass, spilling a slurp of its contents on her academic gown which was tinged with copper sulphate green and evidently of considerable antiquity like its owner.

'Doctor Cornwall,' she cried, a little too loudly, 'I'd like you to meet Professor Trethewey who runs the Department of Oenology.' She gestured at a small forty-something woman with sparrow features and a red bandanna tying down a shock of blonde frizz. 'And this' – she indicated a short, wide man with an impressive black squared-off beard reminiscent of Dr W.G. Grace, the eminent Victorian cricketer – 'is Dr Penhaligon who is a fellow of the college and reader in Green Studies. As you know, Dr Cornwall, Tasmania likes to think of itself as an eco-paradise and Dr Penhaligon is very much at the cutting edge.'

'In more senses than one,' said Professor Trethewey, arching eyebrows which had been pencilled on to her face like a proof correction. She grinned, revealing uneven teeth. The lipstick around her mouth echoed the pencil mark above the eyes. It looked, thought Tudor, as if it too had been stabbed on because she was displeased with the quality of her basic text. Tudor couldn't see why. It was a perfectly agreeable face in a spiky professorial way. Not exactly sexy but quite fun to have around.

'Sorry,' he said, realizing that he had missed an allusion of some kind.

'Cutting edge,' said Dr Penhaligon, 'does not simply refer to my place at the intellectual fulcrum of environmental activity here in Tasmania, Dame Edith was making a word play with my arboreal activities. Axiomatically as it were.'

Tudor must have looked as nonplussed as he felt.

'Dear Tasman here,' said Dame Edith, 'is a demon chopper. He has a way with wood. As you'll discover, Dr Cornwall, ours is, in some respects, still a primitive hunter-gatherer culture which has changed very little since the days of the first settlers.'

Not before time little Brad appeared on the scene. He was carrying a tray with a fullish glass for Tudor and a decanter to refuel the others. They all took advantage. Brad said nothing but looked obsequious.

'I'll give you a tutorial one day, if you'd like.' The ecologist's remarkable beard twitched with what seemed to Tudor's jet-lagged and friend-deprived susceptibility, a mixture of amusement and menace. Rather more of the latter than the former.

'Tasman is an amateur axeman,' said the professor of wine. 'It gets rid of his inhibitions. I know as a Pom that you'll find it extraordinary, but lumberjacking is a major sport here. Bigger than golf.'

'Isn't chopping down trees a bit, well, ecologically unsound?' ventured Tudor, who had already formed a dim view of Dr

Penhaligon. 'It doesn't sound very tree-friendly.'

'Oh you won't catch him out that easily.' Professor Trethewey seemed amused. 'First of all, he mostly attacks dead trees. And then when he does cut down the living he says it's like culling deer or seals. He only kills the poor specimens which aren't worth preserving. If it wasn't for people like Tasman the world's forests would be completely out of control. Isn't that right, darling?'

The great Green sipped and nodded.

Tudor followed suit and there was an almost awkward pause. Luckily conversation flowed all around them. There were between twenty or thirty people in the room. They were of both sexes, most ages and several colours. The only unifying features were the gowns and the sherry.

'You're Ashley's friend,' said Professor Trethewey. Tudor was startled. He had been filling the pause with an appraisal of the SCR's walls which were decorated with portraits of principals past and present. The one of Dame Edith showed her in academic kit of such dreamcoat garishness that it would have shamed Joseph himself. She sat on a garden chair and on the grass at her feet there were two echidnas. Her predecessors were painted in less alfresco situations but the whiskery steel of each sitter transcended all artistic shortcomings. They consituted a *galerie formidable* which no amount of institutional chocolate box portraiture could conceal.

'Yes,' he said, 'I'm Ashley's friend. But he seems to have disappeared.'

'I wouldn't worry,' she said. 'With the exception of Tasman here I can't think of any member of the college better able to look after themselves. Ashley was one of nature's truffle hounds.'

'Was?' said Doctor Cornwall. 'Why the past tense?'

Professor Trethewey frowned. 'I did say "was", didn't ? I wonder why. My name's Jasmine, by the way. My friends call me Jazz.'

She smiled, in an unexpectedly gamine way, but did not explain why she had referred to Ashley in the past tense. Tudor was on the point of repeating the question but Jazz was saved by the bell. The summons to dinner was as commanding as the call of the muezzin. It brooked no hesitation or interruption and left Tudor perplexed and mildly suspicious.

'For what we are about to receive,' said Dame Edith, when the assembled company was more or less silent, 'may the Lord make us truly thankful.'

Tudor was disappointed that the Grace was not in Latin. Or even Greek.

He was seated, as was clearly the custom, between two students, both female and both rather disconcertingly attractive in a tanned, blonde, tennis-playing sort of a way. Antipodean Joan Hunter Dunn. One was majoring in anthropology, the other in dentistry, for which her immaculate teeth were a good advertisement. Tudor found them easy to talk to even though the talk was mostly small even when it moved on to teeth and animals. Professor Trethewey had been placed opposite him and even though during the minestrone (heavy on the carrot) and fried fish (firm textured but unfamiliar) they did not exchange words he sensed that she was watching him from the corner of an eye.

Presently, in a lull, Professor Trethewey leant across the table and asked, conspiratorially, 'Ashley says you share his taste in fine wine.'

'I wouldn't say that,' said Tudor. 'I know what I like but I'd hardly say I was an expert.'

'But you can tell a shiraz from a pinot, chardonnay and viognier?'

Tudor grinned. 'I wouldn't bank on it,' he said. 'I know if something's corked. And I can tell good from bad. I wouldn't go further than that.'

'Ashley told me you had a fine nose.'

'Then Ashley flatters me. Or he's teasing you.'

'Well,' the professor conceded, 'He did say you had a fine nose for a Pom.'

'That sounds more like him.'

'Even so,' she said. She seemed thoughtful. Then she said, 'Tasman and I are having a small tasting after dinner. We and Ashley constitute the college wine committee. As Ashley's not . . . er . . . with us . . . perhaps you'd care to join us in the Bob Hawke Room. Say half an hour's time?'

'Well thank you.'

'Just half a dozen reds and a couple of stickies. All local.'

'I should enjoy that,' he said, as the toothsome dentist passed him a cup of coffee and he returned to small talk.

Moments later, Dame Edith banged a gavel on the table and said another grace. Latin this time, to Tudor's satisfaction.

'*Benedictus, benedicata.*' And everyone filed out in a more or less orderly fashion. The air had grown evening cold and stars started to appear. Looking up, Tudor saw the Southern Cross and Orion upside down. He shivered. Somewhere out there up on the mountain, out in the bush, his old friend would be looking at the same stars.

Or would he?

'Oh, Dr Cornwall,' came the prickly voice of the Principal out of the gloaming, 'The police are anxious for a word. I volunteered tomorrow morning at nine o'clock in my office. Is that all right?'

'Perfectly,' said Tudor.

'Only a detective constable I'm afraid,' said Dame Edith, 'which presumably indicates the level of importance they're attaching to the matter.'

'I'm sure he's perfectly competent,' he said.

'*She* as a matter of fact,' said the Dame. 'A lady detective.'

'How very fashionable,' said Tudor. He had written papers on women in crime, Christie to Cornwell, Miss Marples' heiresses, and other such subjects. His considered opinion was that, given the conservatism of most police forces, female cops were more prevalent in fiction than in real life. But never mind.

'I'll be there,' he said.

CHAPTER SIX

The Bob Hawke room was sepulchral and fusty, dark-panelled and stained-glass windowed. Tasmanian landscapes, both oil and water, hung from a mahogany picture-rail against a three-dimensional wallpaper the colour of old teeth. It reminded Cornwall of the dimmer recesses of the Westminster Houses of Parliament – Pugin pretension overlaid with dust and decay. On numerous occasions he had sat in such surroundings as an expert witness in self-important and interminable enquiries whose findings were banal, self-evident, wrong-headed and inconsequential. Nobody ever acted upon them, unless there were compelling reasons of self-interest.

It was just so this evening. On a long white clothed table there were six bottles of red wine and two slender green halves of what Tudor supposed was sticky stuff – the local equivalent of five puttonyos Tokay or château bottled sweet Sauternes. There were several glasses, two plates of water biscuits, a couple of spittoons.

'Hail, Fellow! Well met!' said Dr Penhaligon, his nose deep in a glass of Yarra Valley magenta.Before Tudor could think of a witty riposte, the Reader in Green Studies continued, 'Listen, mate, the reds are spankers,' and laughed.

'Pay no attention,' said Professor Trethewey, looking up from a deftly executed spit of purple shiraz grenache mourvedre from

McLaren Vale. 'Tasman's quoting. It's a line from one of our leading winemakers. Good eh?'

Doctor Cornwall felt mildly fazed. He liked Australians but you could never be quite sure when they were taking the mick. He was led to believe that they felt the same about Poms.

'In England, the best thing you used to be able to say about a wine was that you would be amused by its presumption,' he said. 'I'm not sure, even now, that 'listen mate, the reds are spankers' is quite the sort of line that's going to appeal to my friends at Berry Brothers.'

He knew halfway through the sentence that he was sounding pompous.

'All the same, I'm sure your reds are right little spankers.'

This, he suspected, only made it worse.

Tasman Penhaligon was looking at him as if he were a sapling ready for the chop.

'Have a glass,' said Jazz. 'The main thing is we want to get that ghastly Wallaby Creek off the college list. We think the Principal has shares in the company. There's no other reason for having it in the house.'

'I had some of their sherry before lunch,' said Tudor. 'It wasn't *that* bad.'

'Not exactly a "spanker" though,' said Penhaligon, pouring him a generous measure from the first bottle.

'What am I drinking?' Tudor asked, eyeing his glass with suspicion.

'They're all blends,' said the Professor of Oenology, 'with an emphasis on pinot. The climate here suits pinot. Soil too. What do you think of A, Tasman?' she asked, turning an enquiring gaze on the bearded ecologist.

'Strong hint of wattle,' said Penhaligon. 'Undertones of yabby, or maybe Morton Bay Bug. Suspicion of Vegemite on the nose, but that turns to chocolate on the palate. Would go with a kangaroo carpaccio. Pie and mash too. I'd give it six out of ten.'

'Hmm,' said Professor Trethewey. 'And what do *you* think, Dr Cornwall? That's A that you're drinking now.'

Tudor frowned, sniffed, scrutinized, swirled, slurped and spat. 'I think I might give it a seven,' he said. 'Good fruit. Colour's OK. It's very nice.'

'There's pencil and paper,' said the professor. 'Just carry on with the work while we talk. Basically we just need to choose one of these little spankers as the official college red. Also one of the two pudding wines. We can get any of them at cost.' She winked. 'Between us, Tasman and I know most everyone in the industry. At least here in Tasmania.'

There was a brief silence while all three made a self-conscious play of serious wine-tasting. Then Tasman Penhaligon said, 'Doctor Cornwall, we have to talk to you about your friend Ashley.'

'Do please call me Tudor,' he said.

'When did you last see Ashley?' asked Jazz Trethewey.

Tudor replied truthfully that he had seen him nine months earlier at the Toronto conference but that he had stayed in contact on the phone and by e-mail on a regular basis.

The professor puckered her lips, more in thought than distaste for the wine.

'How was he in Toronto?' she asked.

'He was fine,' said Tudor. 'Same as always. Played hard, worked hard.'

'You didn't notice anything odd?' asked Tasman. 'Any deviation from the norm?' He spat, professionally but noisily. 'Was old Ashley his usual self?'

Tudor didn't care for his tone.

'What exactly are you implying?' he asked.

Jazz Trethewey obviously sensed trouble.

'I don't think Tasman is implying anything,' she said, silkily. 'It's just that we've been concerned about Ashley and as you're an old friend of his we felt we ought to share our concern.'

Tudor smelled rats.

'What sort of concern?' he asked.

Jazz and Tasman looked at each other conspiratorially, then turned away and concentrated on their wine as if to say that this was a delicate matter and perhaps they had done wrong to raise it.

'Sex,' said Tasman. 'Your friend Ashley was in trouble with sex.'

Tudor felt the odour of rodent intensify. He presumed that the two academics knew of the charges of sexual harassment that had been levelled against his old friend. However, he had no idea whether they knew that *he* knew. His naturally cautious inclination was to say nothing. Or at least as little as possible.

What he actually said was, 'Sex?'

The moment he uttered it he knew that he had got the inflection quite wrong and that he was sounding more and more like a priggish Pom.

'I'm sorry, Tudor,' said Jazz, giving a little *moue* which seemed designed to convey equal measures of sympathy and exasperation. 'But several of the girls in college have complained that Ashley's been making unacceptable sexual overtures. It's looking bad. Both Tasman and I have been aware for some time that there was something unhealthy in Ashley's attitude towards some of the women students.'

'With respect . . .'began Tudor, then wished he hadn't. 'Ashley's a very old friend. That's simply not his style. Quite apart from anything else there's no need. Ashley's extremely attractive to the opposite sex.'

'*Was*, maybe,' said Penhaligon, 'but he's beginning to show his age. Last year's Lothario is this year's Dirty Old Man. My information is that the red wine isn't the only spanker in college.'

'Give me a break!' said Tudor, and then, guiltily, remembered the alleged thief and the disturbing effect she had had on him.

'Do you have the slightest evidence for any of this?' he asked, a slight tremor creeping in to his voice. It was infuriating, but these two seemed to bring out all the old woman in him. It was not like him normally. He was not in the least bit prudish and was known at the University of Wessex as something of a spade-caller. Here, he became more and more of a parodic Pom with every second.

'I'm afraid we do,' said Jazz.

'Such as?' asked Tudor.

'Female students seen coming and going from his rooms at all hours of the day and night.'

'He's a tutor, for heaven's sake. Of course students come in and out of his room.'

'Funny,' said Penhaligon, 'how they always seem to be girls.'

'Who's watching anyway?' asked Tudor. 'Is someone spying on him?'

'Any case,' said the axeman, 'these weren't his criminal studies students. He'd started a new course of what he called Freshmen's Essays. So these were vulnerable first-year students lured to his room on the pretext of writing essays on "the meaning of life" or some such garbage.'

He took a swig of red wine and swallowed without spitting. Tudor suddenly realized that he was two-thirds of the way towards becoming drunk.

'I think Freshmen's Essays are a great idea,' he said. 'Ashley and I were brought up on them.'

'I think they're something of a red herring,' said Jazz Trethewey, who was spitting out every drop of alcohol that passed her lips and who seemed, if such a thing were possible, several degrees on the minus side of sober. Tudor felt that even after a couple of stiff Scotches she wouldn't even be at the limit let alone over it. 'The point is,' she continued, 'that several of the girls had made complaints about Ashley.'

'Like what?' Tudor was on to bottle C. So far they all seemed a bit thin and vinegary, despite what he had said about A.

'Ashley had been making suggestions,' she said.

'About spanking,' said Penhaligon. 'Isn't that what the French call *le vice anglais*. Something you get addicted to in your single-sex boarding-schools. Isn't that right?'

'You're telling me that Ashley's female pupils are suggesting that he asked them to indulge in some form of flagellation.'

'Something like that,' said Jazz, glancing at her colleague with irritation as he took another gulp of spanking red. 'We do have spittoons, Tasman,' she said.

Tudor made a big play of swirling his glass of C and holding it against the white cloth to test for colour.

'I'm sorry,' he said, 'but this all seems extraordinarily circumstantial. What exactly are you suggesting?'

'We can't know for certain,' said Jazz, trying hard to seem sympathetic and understanding, 'But we *have* thought Ashley's behaviour somewhat suspicious. And there *have* been allegations. And he *does* seem to have vanished. And one can't help putting two and two together.'

'You haven't got two and two,' said Tudor with a wintry smile. 'I make three.'

He knew he shouldn't have said it.

'You Poms,' said Penhaligon. 'All the same. Smart-arse, superior.'

'I'm not sure,' said Tudor, 'that I understand exactly what you're getting at. You're trying to tell me that Ashley has turned into some sort of sex maniac; that he has been harassing female students, and that consequently he's done a bunk. All this just as I come on the scene. I can't say that it makes a lot of sense.'

'I think we have to asume that your arrival is purely coincidental,' said Jazz, 'although if things were to come to a head during your stay here then that would compound Ashley's embarrassment. What we are saying is that Ashley has gone off the rails sexually, that he has been behaving in a manner inappropriate to his status; that his chooks were coming home to roost, and he has escaped in order to avoid facing the music. Is that right, Tasman?'

'That's right,' he said.

'Doesn't sound right to me,' said Tudor. 'It seems far more likely that either he has decided to take a quick break, which is unlikely just when he's said he'll meet me at the airport etcetera etcetera. Or that he has got lost in the bush. Or that he has been abducted by person or persons unknown. Possibly even been murdered.'

'That sounds pretty far-fetched,' said Penhaligon.

'Not as far-fetched as the idea that he's taken flight because of a few completely unsubstantiated allegations about sexual groping.'

Tudor was angry.

Penhaligon was drunk.

Jazz Trethewey was emollient.

'Tudor,' she said. 'You don't mind if I call you Tudor, do you? We're not saying the sex stuff is definitely true. But we are saying that it's been alleged. And we wouldn't be being either fair or honest if we didn't tell you about it. You must see that, surely?'

Tudor, aware that he was sounding less than gracious, said that he supposed so.

'But what,' he wanted to know, 'are we to do?'

'I think we just have to wait for him to reappear and face the music.'

'But what if you're wrong?' said Tudor. 'What if he's dead, or lost, or injured, or kidnapped?'

'We don't think he's any of those things,' said Penhaligon.

'But you don't *know*,' insisted Tudor. 'And that's crucial. If any of those things are even remotely possible we have a duty to *do* something.'

'But if your friend's disappearing act is voluntary, then our doing something is the last thing he'd want,' said Jazz.

'That's too many ifs and buts,' said Tudor, spitting out a mouthful of vinegary pinot noir. 'And now, if you'll excuse me,

I'm going to have to go to bed. It's been a long flight and a long day. And by the way, if I were the wine committee I think I'd give all this stuff a miss.'

It was, he knew, a bad-tempered, even churlish, exit line but that was how he was feeling. He did, however, manage to say 'Good-night' and his hosts replied in kind.

None of them sounded as if they meant it.

CHAPTER SEVEN

The policewoman seemed almost as young as the college thief though not as nubile, being short and squat with rust-coloured hair and freckles. When Tudor entered the Dame's office she was sitting on the very edge of one of the capacious armchairs looking as nervous as a student hauled in for a disciplinary hearing.

Her name was Karen. Police Constable Karen White.She wanted to know if Tudor would like to come with her to Parnsip Field Road half way up the Wurlitzer. This was where Ashley's car was parked.

The Dame had no objection. The Dame seemed rather short of temper this morning, as if, suddenly, overnight, the whole business of Professor Carpenter had gone from disturbing to merely tiresome. It appeared to the Visiting Fellow as if she wanted him out of the way. After all, her role in life was researching the echidna and presiding over college affairs. Not impersonating Miss Marple.

'The fresh air will do you good, Dr Cornwall,' she said, with the authority of one who, even at her advanced age, was an accomplished bush walker still sound in wind and limb. 'And I think you should see as much of the state as possible while you're with us. I hear, incidentally, that you weren't taken with any of the wines last night.'

She said nothing about solving crimes or disappearing persons.

Evidently she had been talking to Tasman Penhaligon or Jazz Trethewey. One or other of them had obviously put in a bad word for him. He would have preferred to have Dame Edith on side, as she had seemed the previous day. Given time, he reckoned, he would win her back, but now was not the time.

'No,' he said. 'I have to confess I wasn't hugely impressed. Maybe it was jet lag. Air travel always plays havoc with my taste buds.'

'Is that so?' Dame Edith's smile was wintry. Tudor wondered if either of last night's wine tasters had passed on his true opinion of the Dame's Wallaby Creek sherry.

Outside, Cornwall and the young WPC did not exchange words until they had fastened their seat belts and were heading towards the mountain. The police car was Japanese, regulation white with standard police trimmings. WPC White drove it with exemplary efficiency and economy. Nothing flashy but nothing limp-wristed either.

'So,' began Tudor, 'is this an official police matter?'

'What do you mean, sir?' she asked, changing gear briskly as the gradient steepened.

'I mean are you investigating a crime?'

'There's no evidence to suggest a crime's been committed, sir,' she said, 'but the circumstances seem suspicious. If the professor doesn't show up soon, I guess we'll have to start looking properly.'

'You mean you're not looking properly?'

She grinned. ' "Seek and ye shall find",' she said. 'But if there's nothing to seek you can't find. We can't look properly for a missing person if no person has been declared properly – or officially – missing. It's the rule. Your friend the professor isn't missing as far as the authorities are concerned.'

'Even though he *is* missing?'

'He's only missing as far as you're concerned,' she said. 'Legally he's just not where you want or expect him to be which isn't at all the same thing.'

'You're saying the law is an ass.' Tudor was beginning to like the policewoman. He watched with admiration as she negotiated a steep upward hairpin and accelerated in to a dark avenue of antipodean evergreens. They had only been driving a few minutes yet already the city seemed impossibly distant. There was not a house in sight.

'So how do you define "missing" in Tasmania?' he asked, aware yet again that he was sounding like a pompous Pom.

'Much like you, I guess,' she stalled, 'We're a former colony. Most of our laws and procedures are pretty much like they are in Britain. Or so I've been told.'

'That's not an answer,' said Tudor.

'No, sir,' she agreed, happily.

Cornwall regarded her with an avuncular amusement which fell short of disapproval but was aimed in that direction.

'Technically,' he said, entering academic mode, 'missing means "not found" or "not in its place". Thus, if one says there is a missing page that means that there is a page one and a page three but no page two. There is a presumption that page two should have existed. Perhaps it did once exist and has been torn out or otherwise removed. Perhaps the book was badly bound or printed and it never existed at all. Either way the page is presumed missing.'

'Missing, presumed dead,' she said.

He did not smile. 'That's usually a military usage,' he said, 'meaning "neither present after battle nor known to have been killed or wounded".'

'Like if you have a body you can prove the person's dead?'

'It's not a laughing matter,' he said, huffily.

'I'm not laughing,' she said. 'Only it's difficult to know when someone or even something is really missing. We know that here and I'm sure you know that in Britain. Take your page in the book: there's nothing to say that the book can't just have odd numbered pages. Like a street, say. One side's even, the other side's odd.'

'Now you really are being facetious,' said Cornwall.

'I'm just saying that without a body it's not cut and dried. I mean look at your Lucan. It took years for your law to decide he was "missing" enough for his estate to be settled, for his son to inherit the title, for him to be taken out of the reference books.'

'How do you know about Lucan?' he asked. 'You're far too young.'

'We did him in college,' she said. 'He's kind of interesting. You know if he's living in like South America like some people still say then he's not missing, is he? He's alive and well.'

'But he's still missing from his wife and family and friends. He's missing from his proper place. He's missing from where he's supposed to be.'

'It's a free country,' she said. 'If he wanted to go and live in South America that's his business. Doesn't mean he's missing.'

'Except that he was suspected of murder.'

'That's correct,' she said, skidding round another tight corner and then, a hundred yards later, pulling into a layby on the right, 'Professor Carpenter isn't suspected of murdering anybody. Not yet anyway. Be interesting if he did murder someone though. Missing presumed guilty.' She smiled. 'We're here. That's his vehicle.'

Tudor got out and stretched. The air up here was crisp and cool. They had been climbing steadily ever since leaving the college. The city lay stretched out below them to the left like a relief map. The effect was similar to that which Tudor first noticed from his window in St Petroc's except that being now so much further away the scale was significantly reduced. Another fat bathtub freighter was scudding up the sound at the entrance to the Derwent River. Cars moved up and down the highways like dots. High-rise buildings which might have seemed imposing from ground level, looked stubby and squat. There was a lot of green; the larger squares presumably parks though it looked as if most Hobart houses had big back yards. The steep slopes of the mountain were wild and unpopulated until the white barked gums and the surrounding scrub gave way to suburban sprawl perhaps three or four miles distant, though it was so steep that if a professional soldier had thrown a grenade it would probably have exploded near the first of the suburban villas, and maybe uprooted a camellia or rhododendron in the shrubbery, or caused a tidal wave in the swimming-pool. All the houses on the city fringe seemed to have pools and shrubberies though they petered out towards the centre. It looked a quiet, affluent sort of place. Not a city where you'd expect to find missing persons. It didn't look as if you could easily get lost in Hobart.

Up here on the mountain it was different. Here, already it was wild, untamed, no longer smiling.

'Trust Ashley to drive British,' said Tudor.

The car was a Land Rover, geriatric to the point of being uncertifiable, a short-wheel-based model with a canvas hood, the sort of thing Tudor associated with black-and-white movies set in occupied Europe. Trevor Howard in a duffel coat and a beret. Ashley affected a sort of old colonial machismo which the Land Rover fitted perfectly. Tudor guessed it wouldn't have gone down too well with some of his colleagues. They would have found it affected. Tudor wasn't sure he didn't agree.

'No sign of foul play,' said Karen. 'Just a parked car.'

'Been parked a little longer than you'd expect though,' said Tudor. 'He'd have had a ticket in town.'

'He's not in town,' she said. 'No yellow lines out here. No traffic wardens. No regulations. God's own country.'

Tudor peered through the window. There was an untouched bar of Cadbury's Fruit and Nut on the passenger seat and a banana on the dashboard. The banana was intact too. It looked blackish and unappetizing.

'Did he come here often?' he asked.

'He came up the mountain most mornings,' she said. 'Could have come here; could have gone some place else. The mountain's full of tracks.'

There was a wooden signpost where the gravel layby finished and the bush began. A narrow sandy track ran steeply uphill. The signpost said 'High Falls 5k.'

'High Falls?' said Tudor.

'Famous beauty spot,' she said. 'Nice morning's walk. Just enough of a climb to stretch your thigh muscles and raise the pulse rate. About an hour and a half for someone reasonably fit. Which I understand Professor Carpenter was.'

'Was?' he said sharply.

'Is .. was . . . who knows?' She didn't seem to care much. Policemen and policewomen seldom did in Dr Cornwall's experience. Professional indifference induced by over-exposure to dead bodies. He found it slightly shocking in one so young.

'Does the track end at the Falls?' he asked.

She shrugged and Tudor remarked to himself that she had a cool line in not caring very much.

'Sort of. Most people would just do the round trip. It's a popular gentle walk. But if you want to go on you can walk till you hit the sea which is, I'd guess, about five hundred kilometres away at Wittling Point.'

'Could you do that?' he wanted to know. 'Walk all the way from here to Wittling Point?'

'Sure,' she said. 'It would take a while but there's no reason why not?'

'There's a track?'

'Not what you'd call a track in the UK. But an experienced bushwalker could do it. No problem. Well, he could, but then again maybe he couldn't.'

'How do you mean?'

'Five hundred ks is a long way. You have to carry all you need. There's no settlement after the first fifty or so ks. It's all wilderness area. Designated. Protected. Most people fly in by light plane. If you get sick or break a leg there's no way out.'

'Other than by aeroplane.'

'Yeah, but there aren't many places you can land. Not more than two or three primitive strips all the way between here and WP.'

'So Ashley wouldn't have . . .' Tudor was thinking out loud, an irritating habit of his which had cost him some otherwise rewarding relationships. Women seemed to prefer it if he kept his thoughts to himself which he often did. But not always.

'It's not a picnic. So no way. You don't just come up here one breakfast time and say "hey jeepers, why not take a stroll down to the ocean?"

'So in the normal course of events he'd just wander up to the Falls and wander back again?'

'Guess so. That's what most of us do.'

'Hmmm.'

For a while the pair of them stared at the Land Rover as if willing it to divulge its secret. It obviously knew something they didn't.

'Shall we walk up to the Falls?' he asked, 'I'd like to see them. And you never know.'

Karen shrugged again. Tudor decided it was a habit he might eventually find irritating – if he were ever given the time.

'Sure,' she said.

It was a steep climb but the path was well-defined and firm underfoot. You didn't have to be a Ranulph Fiennes to negotiate it. The scrubby woodland to either side was a different story. It looked impenetrable. Also much of it was higher than he had anticipated. It might not have come up to an elephant's eye but it would have been near head-height on a man of average build. A diminutive policewoman such as Karen would soon have disappeared from sight.

'Easy to get lost in that.' Tudor flicked his head in the direction of the surrounding wilderness.

'People do,' she said. 'Even this close to the city. But not if you know what you're doing. Out there in the wilderness maybe. That's a different story. But someone like your friend wouldn't have any worries here. This is like Regent's Park for a Londoner, Central Park for a New Yorker, the Champs-Elysées for a Parisian, Unter den Linden for a Berliner . . .'

'They teach you that in college?' asked Tudor waspishly.

'Maybe.' The shrug was imperceptible this time but she still smirked.

Tudor was quite fit but the climb was steep, and, he reminded himself, they were at altitude. After a while he didn't trust himself to speak for fear of sounding breathless. That would have meant loss of face. Normally he wouldn't have worried much about that, having the self-confidence to dispense with such feeble vanities, but just now with this irritating Tasmanian police-woman he felt an overwhelming need not to appear weak.

After about half an hour they entered a damp area festooned with ferny fronds and frondish ferns glistening in the damp from a trickling stream. The moisture lent a rheumatic quality to the already chill air. The stones had gathered moss which stained his sleeve a luminous green, once when he stumbled on a slimy sheet of slate and put out a hand to steady himself. After ten minutes or so of this, the path turned into wooden steps carpeted with thin criss-cross wire to prevent further slippage and then at the top of this metal and pine staircase they emerged on to a small viewing platform.

Ahead and above, High Falls fell silver through green foliage into an iridescent pool illuminated by shafts of sunlight beaming through the leaves of gum and fir and knotty mountain oak. She was a very narrow fall like the mercury in a thermometer but high and gleaming in the thin mountain air. Beautiful in a ghostlike way, thought Tudor, and alive with a sodden drip of intangible threat. In daylight there seemed little harm in this sylvan slippery, slimy stream but at night he could imagine a dank mysterious air of water torture. He shivered and not from cold. He had always been more than usually susceptible to a sense of place. And this place had a sense all right. Mystery and menace, mire and mould.

'Ssshhh,' said Karen, unnecessarily, for he was silent as the grave.

He froze and the two of them listened, straining to hear over the trickling sibilance of the falls.

'Animal,' said Karen. 'Dog, I think.'

They listened again and this time Tudor thought he too caught the thin echo of a canine whine over the sound of water falling on rock. Ridiculously he remembered, years ago, seeing a Conan Doyle adventure in a village cinema in southern Spain, the wholly expected but nonetheless chilling bay of *El Perro de Baskervilles* against a backdrop of full moon, meerschaum and deerstalker. The distant whimper in the watery wilderness of the Wurlitzer had a similar effect. His spine felt chilled.

'Up there,' said Karen, pointing halfway up the fall. 'Dog. Sure of it. Let's go look.'

And almost once she was over the pine railing and into the wild scrub, up to her shouders, scrambling and clambering upwards in the direction of the allegedly doggy cries.

Tudor followed, a shade gingerly as befitted a man of his age and station but nimbly enough for all that.

For ten minutes they climbed, then reached a narrow emerald green plateau of mossy grass, little more than a shelf in the steep mountainside. There, tied with a long rope to a slender, evergreen, larch-like tree, was a mottled heavy-shouldered dog, now all bared lip and wagging tail, pleased to see them.

'Blue heeler cross,' said Karen.

The dog wore a metal tag on his collar.

Tudor, a dog person to his fingertips, walked across, knelt, ruffled the heeler's head with the fingers of his right hand and took the tag in his left.

'Basil,' he read out loud, 'c/o Prof. Carpenter, St Petroc's College, Hobart.'

He turned to look up at WPC White.

'Well,' he said, 'do you think we have a missing person now?'

CHAPTER EIGHT

Basil's return to St Petroc's did not go unnoticed.

'What in God's name are you doing with that bloody dog?' asked Dame Edith who was watering roses as Dr Cornwall and WPC White drove into the garden quad. The second Tudor opened the passenger door, Basil leapt out, snarled briefly at the Principal and cocked his leg against an abundant scarlet floribunda.

Dame Edith snarled back.

'I can't think what Ashley sees in that mutt,' she said. 'Where is he anyway? And where's he been?'

Tudor sighed. 'We've found the dog,' he said, 'but not his master.'

'Ashley,' said Dame Edith, 'never goes anywhere without Basil. Basil never goes anywhere without Ashley. They are, in a word, inseparable.'

'Not any more they aren't,' said Tudor. 'Police Constable White and I found the dog tied to a small tree near High Falls about three-quarters of an hour off Parsnip Field Road halfway up the Wurlitzer.'

'I know perfectly well where High Falls is, young man. But where is Professor Carpenter?'

'That's what I am trying to tell you,' said Tudor. Academics were the same the world over, he thought to himself. They never listened to anyone but themselves. 'We found the dog but not Ashley,' he said. 'The dog was on its own. Tied up. Not happy. No Ashley.'

Dame Edith put down the watering can.

'That's not good.'

'No.'

'What's your view, Constable?'

Tudor was afraid Karen was going to do one of her shrugs, but instead she said, 'I don't know yet. I have to report back. Off the record, I'd have to say our investigations will have to be upgraded.' She smiled. 'So I guess I'd better get back to the office. I'll leave you to look after the dog. I don't think he'd be happy in the police pound. See you later.'

She drove away at speed leaving the Principal, the Visiting Fellow and the dog regarding each other warily.

'I like dogs,' said Tudor eventually. 'I'll look after him till Ashley gets back.'

'*If* he gets back,' said Dame Edith. 'Still, I'm obliged. I don't care for dogs. Especially this one.'

She seemed to soften. Indeed, for a moment she seemed almost vulnerable and Tudor was on the verge of feeling sorry for her. Her world was St Petroc's and St Petroc's showed ominous signs of instability. From his own experience at the University of Wessex he was only too well aware of the fragility of academic institutions. The academics disliked other academics, only uniting in their hatred of the all-powerful administrators. Academics and administrators in turn only made common cause when it came to their weary contempt for their students. This, in turn, was heartily reciprocated. There were exceptions to this jaundiced view of Dr Cornwall's but he believed that they only served to prove the rule. He personally had always enjoyed cordial even warm relations with his students, though less so with his colleagues, but he was not usual. In any case, he was old enough to remember the distant days when student revolt had almost destroyed universities. He had seen how vulnerable they could be. Dame Edith would know this better than he which was why she was perturbed.

'It's a worry,' she said.

He agreed.

'What are we to do?'

'Let the police try to find out what's happened. That's what they're for.' Even as he said it Tudor realized that it sounded limp. He also knew that if this had happened on his own home turf he would have taken a more pro-active attitude. In Wessex he had contacts, an understanding of how things worked; he belonged, it was home. Here he was a stranger, out of his depth. He had been relying on Ashley to show him the ropes, explain the procedures, intoduce him to his network. And now Ashley far from solving his problems had become the problem himself.

'In situations such as this I always rely on Professor Carpenter,' she said, sounding prissy.

'Well, in this situation that's hardly an option,' he said, 'and what exactly do you mean by "situations such as this"? I had imagined this was unique but perhaps not. Do members of your senior common room often go missing?'

'I don't think that's funny.'

'It's not meant to be funny. You're telling me that you've had other situations in which you rely on Ashley. I want to know what you mean.'

She picked up the watering can and stared at it as if expecting it to give her inspiration.

'I think you'd better have a word with Lorraine,' she said. 'She can explain the ins and outs of college life. Besides, she and Ashley are friends. That is to say, well it's none of my business and I have no idea exactly what the state of their relationship is. Or was. That's probably beside the point. You must understand that in a society such as this we are constantly having to deal with situations in which, well, I've already told you about our current problems with theft. It isn't the first time we have had to deal with people stealing things. I prefer that when such problems occur we solve them ourselves. If we go outside for solutions there is nearly always talk and careless talk—'

'Costs lives,' said Tudor, wishing he hadn't.

She gave him a sharp look.

'There have been two deaths since I became Principal of this college,' she said, 'and in both cases we have managed, partly thanks to Ashley's common sense and to his influence in all manner of quarters, to avoid unwelcome publicity.I'm sorry that's a tautology. All publicity is unwelcome. The one is synonymous with the other.'

'What sort of deaths?' Tudor wanted to know.

'Let us just say that both were what you might call drug-related. Young people do tend to get in to trouble with drugs. They're also prone to depression. The combination can have disastrous consequences.'

'You forget,' said Tudor, 'that I too work in a university.'

'You're right,' she said, 'I do forget. Too often these days I'm afraid. Age wearies me and the years condemn.'

Tudor was about to say 'I wouldn't say that' but thought better of it. She might be old and batty but she had a keen eye and ear for humbug and hypocrisy. So instead, he asked, 'Lorraine? Tell me more. I don't know about her.'

'Lorraine Montagu,' she replied. 'My ears and eyes. Lorraine is called 'the college secretary' but that does her infinitely less than justice. She is the one who really runs this place. Without her it would all grind to a halt. She is the most efficient person I've ever met. And one of the most sympathetically observant. She says very little but she misses absolutely nothing.'

'And she and Ashley. . . ?'

She sighed. 'I'm too old to know or care about that kind of thing,' she said. 'I can only surmise . . . Oh, please, I'm tired . . . go and organize that wretched dog and I'll talk to Lorraine.'

Organizing the dog was a problematic task. However, despite his snarling disregard for the College Principal, Basil seemed, as far as Dr Cornwall was concerned, eminently biddable. The only real problem was that from somewhere among the shrubs beyond the rosebed he had retrieved a mouldy old lawn tennis ball which he was treating like a cross between a bone and a boomerang, alternately worrying it with a growly wagging of the head and laying it at Tudor's feet, and then retreating so that the Visiting Fellow could throw it away for him to retrieve.

'Ashley must be a softer touch than I thought,' said Tudor. Considering that he had spent a whole night on the chilly Wurlitzer the dog seemed remarkably sprightly. Tudor supposed he had better feed him. The college kitchen would presumably have some scraps. He decided to wander across and see what he could rustle up. Dame Edith had told him he could come and go as he wished and that the catering manager or one of his staff would let him have any basics he wanted such as tea bags, instant coffee, bread or marmalade. There was a modest kitchenette in his quarters and although he was expected to eat lunch and dinner, especially dinner, in college at High Table there was a dispensation over breakfast. Tudor was grateful for this. He was not at his best at breakfast.

The college kitchen was preparing lunch when he got there. A Chinese chef was stir-frying rice dextrously in an industrial-sized wok and sundry students were earning much needed pocket money slicing salad vegetables. One of them looked up and smiled flirtatiously. It was Elizabeth Burney.

'Why, hi!' she said. 'It's Doctor Cornwall. And you've got Basil with you! What have you done with his master?'

'I haven't done anything with his master,' said Tudor, grumpily, irritated to find himself attracted by the girl's slightly brazen sexuality. He liked to think of himself as discreet and sophisticated when it came to women. He wasn't supposed to be turned on by a tarty little number like this. It was like being found ogling a page three girl when he was claiming to be fascinated only by the mature charms and sophisticated conversation of university professeuses.

'That's funny,' she said. 'Basil and Professor Carpenter are usually inseparable. Still, Basil seems to have taken to you all right.'

This was true. The dog had brought the tennis ball with him and kept dropping it between Tudor's toes and backing off in an anticipatory crouching position hoping that he would kick it away so that he could run it to earth and bring it back for a repeat. The ball was already sodden with saliva and almost certainly broke all known health and safety regulations here in the gratifyingly sterile-seeming kitchen.

'I'm looking after him till Professor Carpenter gets back,' he said. 'I think he could use some food and drink. I'll lay in some supplies but I must confess this wasn't something I was expecting.'

'What do you think Basil would like?'

'Meat and biscuits. Water. Maybe a bone.' He smiled despite himself. 'Dogs are pretty basic animals and Basil gives me the impression of being a pretty doggy sort of dog. I'd say he's a meat and biscuit bloke. Bones too. I'd be very surprised if he wasn't pretty heavily into bones.'

Elizabeth nodded. 'Nothing fancy,' she said. 'I'll ask Stephen. I don't think he's going to offer us any of his special fried rice but I'm sure we can manage a basic Basil lunch. Will he eat here or do you want a take-away?'

'I'll need a couple of bowls,' he said, 'So if you can manage a take-away I guess that would be good.'

She nodded and went over to the Chinese chef who paused from his wokmanship, looked over at Tudor and Basil, grinned and nodded, then said something to the girl who nodded and grinned back.

'He says he's got tons of tinned Spam which he keeps for

emergencies like nuclear holocausts and stray dogs,' she said. 'The biscuit will have to be cheese crackers. The water's no problem. Tasmanian tap water's high grade stuff. And there are beef bones in the fridge. He's making stock later.'

'Serious chef,' said Tudor approvingly. 'Please thank him and say I'll introduce myself properly when he's not stir-frying.'

A few minutes later Elizabeth came back with a large plastic carrier bag. 'Two bowls,' she said, 'two cans of Spam, one packet of water biscuits and a dirty great beef-bone. I assume you have access to a tap so you can provide your own water.'

He thanked her in a politely formal way which he hoped would make her think he was probably gay. Basil wagged his tail.

'See you later,' said the girl, and Tudor wondered whether it was just a figure of speech. He had a nasty feeling she might have something definite in mind. She was trouble, no mistaking the fact. Bloody Ashley! He could kill him.

Always supposing he wasn't already dead.

CHAPTER NINE

Basil enjoyed his Spam and water biscuits, slurped down some water and then took his bone into a corner where he gnawed it noisily.

Tudor looked on approvingly. He liked his dogs doggy.

A note had been pushed under the door. It was from Dame Edith.

Lorraine Montagu says she could see you at noon. Please could you be good enough to phone her on 0012. Edith.

He looked at his watch. It was ten to twelve already. Oh well, why not? If she was or had been having a relationship with Ashley she might be able to shed a little light where at the moment he saw nothing but gloom. And if the Dame was right she might be able to give him a better crash course on college life, criminal or otherwise, than he had had so far. Too much shade and not enough light.

He debated whether or not to take Basil along on his piece of rope but the dog looked perfectly content with his bone.

'Stay there and mind the shop,' he said, 'and no crapping on the carpet.'

Basil glanced up and continued chewing.

'Wish he could talk,' murmured Tudor to himself, slamming

the door behind him and taking the stairs two at a time. But even if the dog could go into the witness box what could he say? He would have been bundled into the Land Rover for a morning walk from Parsnip Field Road to High Falls. Perfectly conventional morning constitutional. Then at the Falls Carpenter tethered him to that tree up on the plateau. Basil obviously trusted his master completely so he wouldn't have complained. But if Ashley was continuing on his walk why would he abandon the dog? Basil was a muscular Aussie blue heeler in the prime of life. He would have coped with a strenuous bush walk at least as well as the professor.

In any case, Tudor wasn't convinced that the dog had spent the night on the mountainside. Had he done so he would have been in a much worse state than he actually was. Wouldn't he?And wouldn't he have been found earlier? The track to the Falls was a popular walk and even during the week there would be reasonably large numbers of people. Surely someone would have heard the dog's barks or whimpering. After all he and Karen White had heard him easily enough. So if this line of thought was correct the dog wouldn't have been tethered to his tree until twenty-four hours after Ashley went missing.

And why would Ashley go missing just as his old friend and colleague was arriving from England? It didn't make sense.

The harmless, workaday explanation was that Ashley had driven up the mountain one morning and simply decided on the spur of the moment to carry on walking. But that didn't explain the dog. Nor, really, the mobile phone and the lap-top. You wouldn't encumber yourself like that on a spur-of-the-minute bush-walk, would you? No, it seemed more and more probable to the Visiting Fellow, that his friend had been abducted against his will. His captors had clearly got the laptop and the phone but there was no way of telling whether they or Ashley were sending the e-mails. He sighed. Oh well, early days. He just wished his friend and host would reappear. Quickly.

These thoughts occupied Tudor's mind all the way across to the college office. Inside, a female receptionist in a maroon blazer with a white shirt and a maroon tie that matched the blazer, flashed a dazzling set of teeth and told him that Mrs Montagu was expecting him. He frowned. He didn't know why but he hadn't been expecting a 'Mrs'. The girl motioned him towards a closed door on which he knocked. The answering 'come in' came almost at once and he walked in to a large, light, airy office with some well-stocked book cases, some passable watercolours of eucalyptus landscapes with big sky and far horizons, and a big uncluttered desk with a bowl of mainly red roses that looked freshly cut.

She stood to greet him and Tudor immediately recognised her as 'Ashley's type'. His too, of course. They had always shared similar tastes in women, ever since Miranda all those years ago at Oxford. She was a big-boned athletic type just the attractive side of horsy. Tudor put her in her late thirties, though she could just as well be a mid-forties person who took good care of herself. Her smile was relaxed and natural enough but something about her expression and a slight puffiness made him wonder if she had been crying.

'Doctor Cornwall,' she said. 'How nice. Ashley told me so much about you.'

Tudor smiled. He was on the point of saying something to the effect that Ashley hadn't told him anything at all about her but he didn't. Instead he muttered something mildly fatuous about hoping that Ashley hadn't told the truth. She didn't give the impression of listening, though this wasn't, he thought, through lack of interest. She was clearly sizing him up, but some sort of flak detector had obviously seen an empty pleasantry coming and told her to pay no attention.

She motioned him to one of two capacious armchairs and sat down in the other crossing her legs which were long and agreeably shaped though sensibly surmounted by a tartan kiltish skirt and terminated in stylish but equally sensible black patent leather shoes.

'Dame Edith seemed to think that I could help,' she said.

'She seems to think you have your finger on the pulse of the place,' he said.

She gave a little laugh.

'I used to think that was true,' she said, 'but I'm not so sure any longer. Especially since Ashley . . . since Ashley went off.' Her composure was teetering on the brink. The lips quivered a little and she definitely dabbed at an eye as if wiping away an unwanted tear drop.

Tudor said nothing and a slightly embarrassing silence ensued.

Eventually she broke it.

'You know about me and Ashley?' she said.

'I don't know anything about Ashley and you,' he said, 'but I'm beginning to guess.'

She smiled. 'That's just the sort of thing he would say,' she said.

'So are you going to tell me, or am I going to have to go on guessing?' he asked.

'We've been very discreet,' she said. 'In fact I don't think anyone in the college even suspected. But, well, we're engaged to be married. Just as soon as my divorce comes through. It hasn't been easy I can tell you. Dame Edith is eagle-eyed and she's also a tad censorious. This is a religious foundation as she never tires of telling me. She doesn't approve of relationships between unmarried members of staff and even less when one of them is married to someone else. Which is what I am. I mean, I've been separated for years but technically speaking I'm still, well, married to someone else. So Ashley and I had to keep a low profile.'

Privately, Tudor couldn't help thinking that his old friend would have much preferred it that way. Ashley was, on the whole, a low-profile man. Especially when it came to sex. He guarded his privacy.

'Ashley and I are going to get married,' she said, blushing like a young girl, and Tudor felt like blushing for her. Ashley was even less likely to get married than he himself. Ashley simply wasn't husband material. The phrase 'confirmed bachelor' had acquired a mildly pejorative homophobic connotation which certainly didn't fit Ashley. But in its old-fashioned sense that was exactly what he was. It would have to have been a guileful and single-minded woman who would persuade Ashley Carpenter down the aisle. And he didn't think that was Lorraine Montagu. She seemed too uncomplicated which, he guessed would have been one reason Ashley would have been smitten with her.

'Forgive me,' he said, 'but I understand that Ashley was the subject of sexual allegations made by a number of students.'

She seemed disconcerted though only for a moment. 'Dame Edith told you?'

'Only that. She didn't seem to believe it.'

'I should think not. It's all been got up by that little slut Elizabeth Burney. It's her pathetic attempt to discredit Ashley's investigation of the college thefts. She knew the game was up and this is the only way she can save her skin.'

'Not very nice.'

'She's not very nice.'

'You don't think there's anything in it?'

'Don't be ridiculous. You know Ashley. Quite apart from the fact that molesting students simply isn't Ashley's style, there was no conceivable reason for it. He's being well looked after in that department.'

'Sex?'

She flushed.

'Yes,' she said. 'Sex.'

'I'm sorry,' said Tudor, 'I'm not being prurient. It's just that I'm concerned. In fact I think we're all concerned.' He thought for a moment. 'Am I right in thinking that Ashley was often used by the Dame and the college as a sort of unofficial police force? As a sort of academic investigating authority?'

'You could put it like that. We much prefer to deal with disciplinary matters internally. The last thing we want is the police coming in and—'

'Nasty, boorish, incompetent reactionaries trampling on academic and intellectual sensitivities?'

'I didn't say that.'

'You implied it.' He raised his hands in a placatory gesture. 'I'm not criticizing: it's the way we try to do things at Wessex. Most institutions would like to do the same, don't you think?'

'I think we understand our problems better than any outsider possibly could.'

'We all think that. But you have a particular understanding. One that is denied to others.'

She looked reproving.

'I'm not claiming special powers or abilities,' she said, 'but the nature of my job means I know a great deal about the individual circumstances of our students. If I'm correct my duties are a combination of what in the UK would be performed by the dean and the domestic bursar. I do discipline and I do money.'

'As well as counselling, care in the community, therapy.'

'That's for individual tutors. We have a system of "moral tutors" so each student has his own personal friend in the teaching body. I'm responsible for some people's moral welfare. So is Ashley and Jazz and Brad and Tasman and everyone. It's divided up.'

'But you do everyone's money and everyone's discipline?'

'Subject to council's agreement. We're very democratic.'

'I don't doubt it,' he said, and when she gave him another of her hurt, 'you don't believe what I'm telling you' looks, he repeated what he'd said earlier, that he wasn't being hostile, just trying to find out as much as possible in as short a time as he could.

'What strikes me,' he said, following on this emollience, 'is that if you and Ashley were an item in a personal sense, you must have been a powerful force in the life of the college. You have the knowledge and the executive powers to discipline. Ashley, in effect, has the powers of a private police force with none of the restraints that a real police force operates under in a democratic society.'

'We *are* a democratic society,' she said.

'Don't be silly,' said Tudor, beginning to lose patience. 'Of course you're not. It's not a criticism, just a statement of fact. What makes you and Ashley unusual is that between you, you really have the place sewn up. Getting on the wrong side of you is worse than getting on the wrong side of the law. It's like getting on the wrong side of the Gestapo.'

'That *is* offensive,' she said, 'and unfair.'

'Put it another way,' he said. 'You and Ashley are powerful figures in your own right but as a team you're more than powerful. And that sort of power breeds resentment.'

'No one knows we are a team.'

'I find that hard to believe,' said Tudor, almost adding 'if it's true that you're a team.' Of course he had his doubts. Ashley simply wasn't a team player.

'Was Ashley unpopular?'

She considered this for a while. 'On a personal basis, yes, I'd say very. But you're right. His position did make people suspicious of him. And the new generation don't seem to be as law-abiding as they used to be. And Ashley sets a lot of store by being law-abiding. You have to in a small community like this.'

Tudor smiled to himself. Ashley hadn't been like that when he was a student himself. Age played discomfiting tricks. He wasn't at all sure that young Ashley would have cared for old or middle-aged Ashley. Or vice-versa.

'Putting it bluntly,' he said, 'do you think anyone could have disliked Ashley enough to kidnap him or even to kill him?'

She sniffed.

'Well, yes,' she said, 'I suppose I do.'

CHAPTER TEN

Basil was still at his bone when Tudor returned.

'Knick knack, paddywhack!' said the Visiting Fellow.

The dog glowered.

'I forgot,' said Tudor, 'you're not an English dog, are you, Basil? A lesser breed without the law.'

Basil growled.

Tudor grinned. He was warming to Basil.

He had picked up a meat pie in the St Petroc's refectory. It was hot, tasted faintly of Vegemite and had the same sort of comforting effect on him that he guessed the bone had on Basil. He held it in a thick paper napkin and wiped gravy off his chin reflectively. Basil watched with a suspicion of envy.He also guarded his bone with a baleful watchfulness which conveyed the impression that he thought Tudor might nick it from under his damp black nose once he'd finished with the meat pie.

Why on earth, wondered Tudor yet again, would Ashley have abandoned a dog like Basil half way up the mountain? It was totally mysterious. In fact, that was beginning to seem the most plausible motive: a desire to create mystery. The whole affair was some sort of sick joke. His old friend had flipped. Some form of male menopausal dementia had overcome him. He was no longer himself. He was playing some sort of game by Kafka out of Lewis Carroll.

'I suppose,' he said half to Basil and half to himself, 'there's going to be another damn-fool e-mail on the machine.'

He swallowed the last of the meat pie, walked acoss to his laptop and switched on, watching irritably as the screen flickered the interminable graphics, hieroglyphs and jargon which it apparently had to rehearse before doing anything useful.

After what seemed like an eternity, he clicked on to his internet server and was unsurprised to find the legend 'You have 1 Message' staring at him from the bottom left-hand corner. He did not have to be the last of the great detectives to guess who it came from. Or who it *purported* to come from. He clicked again and watched and listened as the computer dialled the local access number with a staccato series of bleeps which merged into a fuzz of static accompanied by the single word 'Connected'.

'If only,' he muttered. 'Connected' was exactly what he wasn't. He was profoundly and disturbingly disconnected.

Hi, Tudor, he read, *Sorry but I almost forgot. I understand you have already embraced the oenological side of college life but I don't know if you've clocked the mulled wine competition. There's a pleasant Petrocian tradition of wassail and mince pies with reedy minstrels and carols on Twelfth Night. Not a tradition at all, of course, scarcely even a habit. Just another effort to persuade the natives that they are still umbilically attached to Mother England. Every year the Fellows compete to see who will have the honour of mixing the negus. I'm rather keen to win this year since the prize has been monopolized by Penhaligon and Jazz Trethewey in recent years but it looks as if I'm not going to be able to be actually present.*

Would you stand in for me, old sport? The recipe and all the spices and so on are all in the top right drawer of the writing-desk in my room. Staircase four in the Tower Block. Just mix in proportion to the wine. Any old plonk will do. A box of Cab Sav or Shiraz for preference. Stick with the formula though – it's an Oxonian conceit, seventeenth century except for the dried wattle which is an Antipodean touch. Definitely no coarse sugar. The little golden balls are an essential refinement. Your new wine buff friends will tell you the rules and all that. It's a blind tasting and the Principal decides though all the Fellows have what is called an 'advisory' vote. Quaint eh?

'Did I say Lewis Carroll?' said Tudor. 'Or did I say Kafka?'

If the rather arch, half-parody of an ancient Oxford don's writing style was not Ashley himself, it was a very clever imitation. Tudor was inclined to be convinced. In which case he wished the hell he knew what he was playing at.He supposed he had better check Ashley's desk. There didn't seem to be any alternative so he told Basil to stay where he was and went off to investigate.

He located the Tower Block without difficulty for it was literally named and appeared to be the only tower in the college. It was Victorian Gothic, red brick, five storeys high and surmounted by a Big Bennish clock: a sort of colonial campanile. The rooms were identified in Oxbridge style at the base of the staircase with white Roman numerals followed by the name of the inhabitant. There were no christian names, merely initials followed by surnames, and there was no way of telling the sex of the various students. Ashley's room or rooms did not have a number. His legend read *Penthouse. Prof. A. Carpenter*.

Tudor, fittish, took the stairs two at a time and arrived on the top floor not remotely out of breath. The door was locked and he had no key but although he was a theoretical rather than practical student of crime and criminals, he did have a reasonable grasp of the basic essentials. A deft manoeuvre with his American Express card yielded an almost immediate dividend and he slipped easily into his friend's lofty suite. He would, he often told himself, have made a perfectly respectable petty thief. It was a comforting thought especially as university life became more and more cut-thoat and penny-pinching. He could sometimes almost envisage a time when crime would come to pay more than criminology.

The drawing-room or study was bookish and austere, minimally furnished and decorated in a manner which said little or nothing about the occupant beyond the fact that he was happy to go along with whoever was resonsible for the design and decoration of the St Petroc rooms. Presumably some sort of domestic bursar.

The books were evidence of wide professional reading: row upon row of green Penguins; studies of crime fiction by the likes of Keating and Symons, bound volumes of the *Strand Magazine*, a first edition of *The Moonstone* and then, of course, at least double that amount of real life crime: Capote and Burn, the Yorkshire Ripper, the Moors Murderers, Crippen, Bodkin Adams and endless volumes on criminal psychology, forensic dentistry, the pathology of patricide and what looked like a complete set of the journal of the Royal Institute of Criminal Affairs.

The desk itself was almost disturbingly tidy: a small desk-jet printer, a jarful of writing utensils, a Sellotape-dispenser, a blotter, a pad of typing paper, a note-pad headed 'Interpol '88' and a pencil sharpener with a crank-handle. All straight lines. No muddle. And a gap where the lap-top must have been.

Tudor smiled. Some things never changed.

The desk was standard college issue, though don-sized, having three drawers a side and a long narrow one in the middle. It was not as big as the Victorian partner's desk which Tudor affected at Wessex, but it was big enough to accommodate the sort of mess that Ashley never made.

There were no locks on the drawers and the top right eased out smoothly enough revealing exactly what the e-mail had said it would. The quantities were a heaped teaspoon of nutmeg, ginger, cinnamon and dried wattle per litre. Also, a sliver of tamarind, an orange and six golden balls. The golden balls were roughly the size of marbles and the label on the packet said they came from a Carthusian monastery in the Auvergne. The prime ingredient appeared to be royal jelly which was often thought of simply as honey but which Tudor knew was a substance secreted by the pharyngeal glands of worker bees and fed to all larvae when very young, but later only to those larvae destined to become queens. Hence royal. It was ambrosial stuff. It was unsurprising to find monks making it, not just because it was heavenly food of the gods but because monasteries often seemed to exhibit apiarian tendencies. Tudor had never heard of anyone putting it in mulled wine but if Ashley was trying to win a competition he could see that it would be an unusual secret ingredient. It would also impart the desired sweetness as well as doing so in a politically correct, organic, non-synthetic manner. Very Ashleyish.

He smiled despite himself and put the spicy ingredients into an empty plastic carrier bag hanging conveniently from a hook on the bedroom door. Then he gazed around hoping vaguely for clues, but there was nothing. It might have been helpful if there were signs of a struggle or a half-eaten sandwich or a glass of whisky waiting to be finished. But there were none of these things, nothing to say whether the room's owner had planned to go away at all, nothing to suggest whether he intended to return. Like its owner it was a room which played its cards close to its chest.

Ashley had always been like that. Tidy in mind and body and with a strong sense of no-go areas. 'Keep off the grass'. Tudor realized that the present peculiar circumstances were making him think about his old friend more than he had done since they were students together. Maybe more. You didn't think about friends when you were at university. You took them or left them, liked them or loathed them. But you didn't subject them to searching analysis. Girls perhaps. Well, no. Not actually. You agonized about what the girl really felt about you but you didn't give much thought to the girl's essential character. In shameful retrospect Tudor had to concede that the nearest most of them had got to understanding the female mind was wondering whether or not the girl would go to bed with them. He sensed that this was more or less reciprocated, but still, in the light of what had happened to the sexes in the intervening years, he was embarrassed by the memories. Genuinely so. He was not an unpleasant person, but no one had taught him anything about women. Like most of his generation he had had to find out for himself. And he was still learning.

The men you took for granted. Provided he stood his round of drinks, didn't nick your girlfriend, lent you his essays and notes in moments of crisis, and could make up a game of agricultural tennis and squash, or basic bridge or poker, you didn't ask much of a mucker or mate. It was astonishing, when you came to think about it, how little you knew about men who were regarded by everyone, including yourself, as a best friend.

Suddenly he was beginning to think this about old Ashley. Good old Ashley. They were best mates, weren't they? Had been ever since Miranda had brought them together. But when it came down to it what had they really got in common? Once it had been Miranda. Or, more accurately, *not* Miranda. Other than that it was blood and beer. Metaphorical blood and literal beer. For most of their adult lives he had been at Wessex and Ashley at Tasmania. Opposite ends of the world. Cards at Christmas; a conference once or twice a year; an occasional learned confabulation to do with forensic dentistry or Sherlockian semantics. It was assumed by themselves and by the world at large that there was much more to their relationship than these flimsy ties. There were bonds that were not articulated. The concept, dignified in the Antipodes as mateship, was not something you discussed. It was a given. A state of mind. Perhaps this was because when you did stop to examine its structure it was so often as a house of cards built on sand.

Thus did Tudor muse, in the tidy set of rooms on staircase four of the old Tower Block, as he clutched his peculiar bag of sugar and spicy tricks. Suddenly he found himself wondering if the man he assumed he knew better than practically anyone in the world was someone he really knew at all. Perhaps he was about to mull wine for a perfect stranger.

The thought was oddly disturbing. He didn't like negus or glühwein anyway. He sighed, and shrugged, and let himself out of a room grown strangely chilly.

CHAPTER ELEVEN

As part of his visitorship – or was it a residency? – Tudor had been assigned classes and pupils. His first was 'Meaning and Murder – the socio-political structure of rural crime in the Golden Age' which translated out of academic language, meant a study of English crime novels by writers such as Agatha Christie and Dorothy L. Sayers in – more or less – the 1930s.

Tudor was pretty good at this though the subject bored him. He wasn't bored by the books themselves, but he was exasperated by the way in which his fellow academics dealt with them. He tended to think of them as detective stories, where his peers and rivals regarded them as texts.

The mysterious disappearance of his host had taken his mind off such matters but, as those involved in criminal matters constantly averred, there was life after death. It went on. When you dealt, as Tudor did, with the daily snuffing out of human existence, often in unexpected and violent circumstances, you ran the risk of becoming inured to shock, bereavement and tragedy. For most people, he used to tell his students, death comes relatively seldom before, inevitably and inexorably, it comes for us all. For the average person death comes but once a lifetime but for those of us who have chosen this path of study it comes disturbingly often.

There were twenty-seven bodies in Room 0731 (b) of the

Menzies Memorial Teaching Block all of them more or less alive. They had that disturbing look of students who were hoping to be able to hang on to his every word. At moments such as this the sexist and probably apocryphal words of Dr Leavis crept unbidden to his mind. Confronted with a Cambridge lecture hall containing a mixed audience, Leavis was supposed to have opened his remarks with 'Good morning, gentlemen. Ladies, have you got that down?'

Tudor had no such prejudices about the female sex – rather the reverse. But he did have misgivings about modern students. When he was their age he had taken everything his tutors said with salt – usually much more than a pinch. In this attitude the best of his teachers positively encouraged him. He remembered A.J.P. Taylor on cold, dank mornings in the examination schools arguing with absolute conviction that Germany was responsible for the First World War and then maintaining just as fervently the following week that it was all the fault of the British. Questions, questions: that was what his education was about. Nowadays all anyone seemed to want was answers.

He sighed out loud and the poised pencils of the 'Meaning and Murder' class gave a collective Pavlovian twitch much as he imagined Leavis's ladies might have done.

'I'm Tudor Cornwall,' he said, 'and as you may already have guessed I come from England. I'm English.'

One or two of the class tittered.

'Now I know,' he continued, 'that we have come here to study fiction but I want to begin with the notion that there is no such thing as absolute fiction any more than there is such a thing as absolute fact.'

Oh dear, he thought to himself, as the writing implements in front of him hovered indecisively above blank paper. He was sowing doubt where he was supposed to be bestowing certainty. But what would criminal studies be without doubt, uncertainty, suspicion and dispute? No conviction, to his mind, was ever wholly safe, no verdict indubitably sound.

'For example,' he said, 'I was invited here by Professor Carpenter. Now you see him, now you don't. One minute he is here and the next minute he is not. Is Professor Carpenter fact or fiction? Is he a figment of our imagination? Or is he as much flesh and blood as you and I? If he is not with us, does he therefore cease to exist? Is his reality dependent upon his physical presence? Or does his absence render him non-existent?'

He paused and smiled. The class was not happy. They were still, several minutes after his first utterance, completely noteless.

'OK,' he said, sighing inwardly. 'How does the Golden Age Mystery traditionally begin?'

He scanned the class with little hope. Some looked blankly back. Others stared at the floor. Surprisingly, however, a hand was raised in the back row. He realized with a stab of something not unlike dismay that it belonged to Elizabeth Burney, the alleged college thief. The tarty alleged college thief.

'Yes,' he said, 'Elizabeth . . . how do you think the typical Golden Age Mystery begins?'

'With a corpse, Professor.'

'I'm not a professor, I'm a . . . well, it doesn't matter what I am. You may call me Tudor. All of you. All of you may call me Tudor. And yes, Elizabeth is right. The convention of the Golden Age Mystery is that either at or very close to the beginning, we are presented with a dead body, a corpse, a cadaver, a stiff, a carcass. There are occasional exceptions to this rule, but for the time being and as this is a first year class we will accept that, yes, Rule One of the Golden Age Mystery, is a dead body on or around the first page. Corpseless crime, at least in the Golden Age, is a postgraduate area of study.' The students who had been scribbling assiduously as soon as Tudor had confirmed that Rule One was a Corpse, came to an abrupt and apparently perplexed halt.

'I'm sorry.' He passed a sweaty palm over his greying hair,

'Joke. Just my little joke.' He must not do jokes, he reminded himself. Particularly to first-year students. Particularly abroad. Jokes to first year students always misfired. Or rather his jokes to first-year students always misfired.

'So, yes. Rule One. A body. Habeas corpus. You must have a body. No, don't write that down. Habeas corpus means something different. Latin. We'll come to that later. Rule One. A body. A dead body. However, in a book of this kind, the body is not just dead it is something else. What else is it apart from dead?'

He looked round the class again. Elizabeth Burney was looking arch and know-all but she didn't put up her hand. The others were all struck dumb, though it was difficult to tell whether this was from shyness, ignorance, stupidity or boredom. He must stop being so cynical, he thought, but he had a horrible feeling it was a bit of all four. 'Right,' he said, 'let us assume that you are one of the great dames of classical crime literature – Dame Agatha Christie perhaps, or Dame Ngaio Marsh, and under no circumstances to be compared with later mistresses of the genre who came to be rewarded with baronies rather than damedoms, such as Baroness James or Baroness Rendell . . .' Oh God, he thought to himself. That's not even a joke, it's a knowing remark, incomprehensible to Tasmanian freshers. Oh well . . .

'Let us simply assume,' he said, sounding desperate, 'that you are writing one of these books. You begin with this body but because of the nature of the book you are intending to write, the body in question has not just fallen under a bus or succumbed to a heart attack or even a mysterious illness. Will it? Well, will it?'

A hand was raised. He knew even before he focused on it that it would belong to Elizabeth Burney.

'Yes,' he said. 'Tell us how this body came to be dead.'

'It was murdered,' she said, a touch coy. 'Unlawfully killed by a person or persons unknown.'

'Good,' he said, 'Good. That is it in a nutshell. We are talking here about murder mysteries and the beginnings of such books are remarkably similar. They open with a body which has been killed in mysterious circumstances. That is the nature of the book.That is, if you like, part one of the formula. It is not enough to begin such books with death. The death concerned must be unexplained and, of course, the purpose of the book is, at least in part, to unravel the mystery. This is why these novels came to be known, colloquially, as whodunnits.'

Elizabeth Burney's hand was up again.

'I don't quite understand,' she said. 'In a murder mystery do you *have* to have a murdered body at the beginning of the book?'

'In the sort of Golden Age whodunnit we're discussing in this class, yes you do.' Tudor felt on firm ground here, but he had to admit that the child was disconcerting. No matter how certain he felt about what he was saying there was something about her which induced uncertainty. She gave the impression of knowing more than he did. Or of knowing something that he didn't. Something significant. It gave an edge; a superiority. It was disconcerting in one so young.

'But in real life that's not necessary?'

'Not necessarily, not in real life, no. But,' he smiled wearily, 'we're not talking about real life here. This is something quite different.'

'So the Golden Age whodunnit has nothing to do with real life?'

'Um . . . no, not a lot . . . that's why they've become unfashionable. Later crime fiction relies heavily on realism. Golden Age stuff is judged largely on the intricacy of the puzzle. The Golden Age authors were playing guessing games with their readers.'

Tudor was aware that the rest of the class were aware of a subtext here although their air of perplexity suggested that they didn't know exactly what the subtext was.

'Don't real-life criminals play guessing games?' she wanted to know. 'Like with the police? The murderer against the detective.

The murderer has to see how many people he can kill before the police catch up with him. The really clever murderer never gets caught. Just goes on killing for ever and ever and no one can catch him. Wasn't that what happened with your Jack the Ripper? And he was before your Golden Age, wasn't he? Wasn't he supposed to be some Pom king?'

'The Duke of Clarence actually,' said Tudor stuffily. He was aware that he was losing control of the situation. He was all for participation, but he was the teacher.The authority was with him. Too much argument and participation led to anarchy. There must be order in the classroom. He represented that order. Law'n'order. The battle cry of the old English Conservative Party as it bayed for hanging and flogging at party conferences from Blackpool to Bournemouth. What was this girl playing at? Just what *was* her game?

'So,' he said, 'the classic whodunnit begins with a murdered body . . . now what comes next?'

He looked round the class.

'Anybody except Elizabeth.' He laughed but it was no joke. Everywhere else he saw apathy or ignorance. Or maybe they were just shy. In any event it was clear that he was going to get no help from any of the other students.The girl knew that too. He sensed her laughing at him though she kept a stern, tight-lipped poker face. There was laughter in her eyes though it reflected a tormenter's pleasure. There was no innocent fun there. Far from it.

Oh well, if he was going to assume the role of old-fashioned schoolteacher, he had better do so properly. He turned to the white board behind him, picked up the black felt-tip pen and scrawled 1) Corpse. 2) Detective.

'It's a little like the Marxist dialectic with which you will, of course, be familiar. Thesis . . . antithesis. And in the crime novel, corpse . . . detective . . . leading ultimately to solution, the denouement in the library, Hercule Poirot or Lord Peter Wimsey reveal all. Can anyone name me a famous fictional detective?'

Silence. Quite an aggressive one. What was the Visiting Fellow there for if not to give them the answers to questions such as this?

'I've just given you two names.'

He was becoming irritated. Mistake. It showed.

'Hercule Poirot and Lord Peter Wimsey are two of the most famous fictional detectives in the history of criminal literature. Poirot is the creation of Dame Agatha Christie and Lord Peter Wimsey is Dorothy L. Sayers's hero.'

'Would they have been successful in real life?'

It was her again, of course.

'Possibly not,' he said. 'Fiction is very different from real life.'

'Yes,' she said. 'That's what Professor Carpenter always said. Just because you can deal with murder in books, doesn't mean you can deal with murder in real life. Or any sort of crime, come to that. Disappearance, kidnap, rape, blackmail.' She got up and gathered her books and papers. 'Sorry,' she said, 'I have to go to work. There's a special function at the restaurant. See you later. You should come. It's a reading sponsored by the Writers Centre and the Yabby Creek Winery. There's a Les Murray look-a-like-sound-a-like who has to be seen and heard to be believed.'

And then she was gone leaving the Visiting Fellow as stunned as his class.

CHAPTER TWELVE

The Meaning and Murder Class had anti-climaxed after the departure of Elizabeth Burney and he was glad to escape back to the growling Basil and the sanctuary of life behind a locked door. He had, however, made a detour and stopped at the grog shop behind the nearest pub, a pseudo-Irish joint called the Doctor O'Reilly, where he had purchased a box of cheap Jolly Jumbuck Central Australian Shiraz Merlot which he thought sounded just about the right base for Ashley Carpenter's cinnamon, wattle and royal jelly witches' brew.

'What's your master playing at?' he asked the dog, after he had poured a glass of Jumbuck and sipped. It wasn't bad.

He decanted a measure he guessed to be as near as dammit to seventy five centilitres into a saucepan and lit one of the gas-rings. Then he added Ashley's various ingredients spoon by spoon. Presently the brew began to steam and a not unpleasant aroma rose nostrilwards. Tudor presumed the unfamiliar slightly musky smell was wattle.

'Well, Bazza,' he said, 'this has the sweet smell of success. I can't imagine Jazz Trethewey or the Penhaligon axeman producing anything with a better nose.'

The dog regarded him with canine disbelief. Tudor found himself wondering whose side he was on and suddenly realized the implication of the query. 'Whose side?' What did he mean by 'two sides'? Did he think that he was on one side and Ashley on the other? He wasn't supposed to be on a side. He was an honoured guest and if this role had changed it should have turned him into an impartial investigator not somebody who was either on- or off-side. Yet as he pondered all this he realized that he did feel as if almost without realizing it he had been put into an adversarial situation. He had enemies in Tasmania; people who were out to get him. And Ashley Carpenter, wittingly or unwittingly, was part of the plot.

He stirred the pot with a wooden spoon. The smell was an odd amalgam of new and old world.

'What do you think, Basil?' he asked, as he took a taste of the spicy mixture. 'Is someone out to get me?'

The dog looked up at him and gave him a half-hearted grimace as if to say Why ask me, sport? but he also, to Tudor's clearly fevered imagination, seemed to suggest that he was a dog who knew more than he was letting on.

Tudor sat down heavily in an elderly leather-upholstered armchair.The warm punch puckered his lips. It needed more royal jelly ampoules. Or maybe they hadn't dissolved properly yet.

Perhaps he should just cut loose and go home. Ashley was the only real reason for his being here and without him he would be better off home at Wessex U. On the other hand, if Ashley had vanished he had an obligation to help find him. Didn't he? That was what a Golden Age detective would have thought, but the Golden Age was dead and gone even if it had ever been alive. In the modern age of gritty professionalism, Tudor, despite his immaculate academic credentials and qualifications, would have qualified as a rank amateur. A salaried, full-time policeman would regard him as a mere diversion. In the 'good old days' people like Tudor would have pulled rank over uniformed coppers or even serious CID officers in belted macs and trilby hats. Not any longer.

'No place for me here, eh, Basil?' he enquired of the dog, who cocked an ear but said nothing. Behind him the witches' brew on the stove was coming to a boil.

He went over and took another sip. Mmmm. The raw, vinegary taste had evaporated, replaced by something sweeter, pungent and almost palatable. He was contemplating the balance of flavours and the emphases of taste when there was a knocking at the door.

Basil barked.

Tudor opened up.

It was Jazz Trethewey, the Professor of Oenology. She was clutching a bottle of Rockford Sparkling Black Shiraz and looking contrite.

'I came to say sorry,' she said. 'May I come in?'

Tudor hesitated, then decided that graciousness was the better part of suspicion.

'Of course,' he said. 'I can't think what you have to apologize for but, please come in. Your peace-offering looks exceedingly acceptable. And I'm a sucker for being said sorry to. Doesn't often happen.'

She laughed a throaty, booze-fuelled laugh and stepped over his threshold.

'I *am* sorry,' she said. 'I've been thinking. We've not been exactly welcoming. In fact, we must seem very rude. It's not intentional and it's certainly not personal. Do you have glasses?' Then as he hesitated she went on, 'I know you have glasses. I know this apartment a lot better than you do. Visiting Fellows come and Visiting Fellows go but I go on for ever. Well, indefinitely.'

She zoned in on the correct cupboard, extracted two large wine glasses, set them down on the dining-table, extracted the cork with a couple of quick twists (the bottle revolving, the cork remaining static in the prescribed manner), poured, took one, gave the other to Tudor, clinked hers against his and said '*Salud*!' then quaffed and sat down in the other armchair.

'So,' she said, 'I'm sorry. By the way, what have you got on the boil over there? Bubble, bubble toil and trouble. Makes a change from scribble, scribble, Mr Gibbon. But what is it? Smells quite choice.'

'Mulled wine,' said Ashley, discomfited. He did not know what to make of this visit. Was she a Tasmanian bearing gifts, or was this a genuine olive branch? Too soon to tell.

'I always say if you can't drink it, don't mull it. More to the point, if you *can* drink it, certainly don't mull it. If wine's good enough to drink then you should drink it *au nature*, but if it's not good enough to drink no amount of sugar and spice is going to make it drinkable. But then I'm something of a purist in these matters. Only to be expected. You can't be expected to hold a chair in oenology and be anything else. But why, if I may ask, are you mulling?'

'I'm entering a brew for the college competition,' he said.

'Oh.' The professor looked thoughtful. 'I don't want to, as it were, resume hostilities, or seem anything other than contrite and agreeable, but how did you know about that? The college mulled wine competition? You've only been here five minutes.'

'Ashley and I discussed it,' he said. 'And I happen to have a rather special recipe.'

Were these lies or half-truths? He wasn't sure but he didn't feel like telling Jazz Trethewey whole truths. Not yet anyway.

'Well,' Jazz smiled without much conviction, 'I don't believe we've ever before had a Visiting Fellow who went in for the competition. I can't say I'm entirely in favour of it. As you will have inferred I regard it as a form of vinous prostitution. But there you are. You probably think me a terrible prig.'

'No,' said Tudor. It was precisely what he had been thinking but he was certainly not going to say it out loud. Not in a moment of truce, however tentative.

'If you're so disapproving then what keeps the tradition going? If it *is* a tradition.'

'That's exactly what the Dame would like to think it had become. A tradition. Dame Edith is an extreme traditionalist as you may have gathered. In all things. She thinks mulled wine is the sort of stuff the dons drink in All Souls, Oxford, or at those Cambridge feasts Tom Sharpe writes about. She sees St Petroc's as a sort of Oxbridge-in-exile. Your friend Ashley is somewhat similar, though more complicated. Most of the Fellows here incline to the Dame's point of view. They wouldn't be here otherwise.'

'But you . . . you're different?'

'Up to a point. The chair in wine is a university appointment, but the way it works is that it carries a St Petroc's Fellowship with it. Just like Oxford or Cambridge. And Fellows are offered rooms in college. I'm not married; the rooms are comfortable; there's tolerable company. It suits me.For now anyway.'

She smiled. More warmly this time. Tudor was struck, as before, by an unexpectedly gamine quality. The red bandanna, the deliberately frizzy hair and the aggressively applied make-up seemed even more than on their earlier meeting like a conscious attempt to obliterate softness and femininity in favour of a sort of academic bohemianism which was as *passé* in its way as all this pseudo-Oxbridge behaviour.

He sipped the fizz. It was good. Also a surprisngly bright blood red. He nodded appreciatively.

'It's from Rymills in the Coonawara,' she said. 'They call it the Bee's Knees. Twenty-two per cent 1998 Cabernet Sauvignon, five per cent 1997 Cabernet Sauvignon, twenty-four per cent 1998 Merlot and forty-nine per cent 1998 Cabernet Franc. The earlier version was about a third Cab Franc and two thirds Shiraz.'

'Ah.'

'It must be tricky coming in to a tight community like ours,' she said. 'And being a Pom you're a double outsider. I'm afraid we haven't helped. We've given off bad vibes, been all prickly like one of Dame Edith's echidnas.'

'Oh, I wouldn't say that. Academics spend a lot of their time being parachuted into other academic communities. I'm no exception.'

'But we're not like *other* academic communities,' she said. 'St Petroc's is a place apart. At least I think it is. It's *sui generis*.'

'All interesting communities think that,' said Tudor. 'It's a symptom of self-respect. What makes this situation awkward is the mystery of Ashley.'

'But the rest of us don't see that there is any great mystery,' said Jazz. 'He's just gone walkabout. People do that down here. It's a national characteristic and a free country. We don't have to account for our movements every second of our lives. We allow each other space, freedom to do what we want with our lives and time.'

'This is getting philosophical,' said Tudor. 'Surely the point about being part of a community, *any* community, is that you have obligations to the other members. You can't manage society if people don't conform to certain understandings.'

'But we don't *manage* society as you put it. We believe in freedom not regulation.'

Tudor sighed. He was tempted to come clean and tell Professor Trethewey about the e-mails purporting to come from his old friend but a still small voice warned against it. Was he being paranoid? Maybe. But trust, to his way of thinking, had to be earned.

'I think that's over-simplistic. I'm as committed to individual freedoms as anyone. I just think people should consider their friends and neighbours. It's basic politeness really.'

'But what if your friend Ashley just needs some space and has gone off to find some peace and quiet?'

'I don't think he'd do that without telling the rest of us. Especially without telling me. I'm coming half way round the world at his express invitation and he said he'd meet me at the airport.'

This time Jazz allowed her smile to upgrade into a short snort of laughter. Slightly derisive laughter.

'Isn't that a bit childish? Everything has been taken care of. You were met at the airport, escorted to the college, shown to your rooms, given a class to teach. Your friend is going through a mid-life crisis and has gone away to sort himself out, but all you can do is to complain that he isn't here to nanny you.'

Put like that his behaviour did sound childish. Tudor could see that. He, however, wouldn't have put it like that. Instead of saying so he put his hands up in mock surrender and said, 'I thought you were bringing a peace offering.'

'I'm sorry,' she said. 'I didn't mean to seem adversarial.' She sniffed. 'It goes against all my prejudices but that concoction of yours is smelling almost appetizing. Is there wattle in it?'

'Yes,' he said.

'How imaginative!' She smiled. 'I wouldn't have thought a Pom would know about wattles.' She sipped her sparkling wine and regarded him evenly over the rim of her glass. Nothing was said but it was clear that she believed that he was holding out on her, keeping something back. The silence was a clear invitation for a confidence but Tudor resisted so that eventually she broke it by saying, 'You're only just in time though. The contest is tonight. Bob Hawke room again. Or did you know that?'

He shook his head. 'No, I didn't know.'

'We only decided this morning. There didn't seem any reason for telling you. We didn't think you'd be entering. As I say, it's not usual for Visiting Fellows.'

'Well, I'm not usual for a Visiting Fellow.' It was his turn to smile.

'*Touché*,' she said. 'So tell me about it.'

CHAPTER THIRTEEN

Sammy was in charge of arrangements for the mulled wine competition. Not long after Professor Trethewey departed, leaving behind an empty bottle of Rymill's Sparkling Bee's Knees and a confused Visiting Fellow, Sammy came knocking in a resplendent scarlet turban and the sort of oriental frock-coat that Tudor associated with the officers' mess of a superior Indian Army Regiment somewhere like Poona. Sammy carried a capacious thermos flask into which he asked Tudor to pour his blend once it was brewed to his satisfaction. If the Fellow sahib would kindly be bringing his flask with him Sammy would be ensuring that it would be decanted in the manner most appropriate. Actually Sammy did not speak in burlesque Punjabi but perfectly straightforward Australian or Tasmanian English even to the extent of prefacing his remarks with a ritual 'G'day' ('G'day, Professor' as a matter of fact). However his appearance and demeanour meant that Tudor *felt* as if he were talking like that. It was a clear case of appearances being deceptive. Because he looked the way he did, Tudor, and nearly everyone else, presumed that he spoke in matching tones. He didn't. It was the sort of behavioural oddity that Tudor liked to include in his lectures.

The thermos was tartan rather like the flasks that Tudor remembered from the beach picnics of his childhood. It was a tartan belonging to no known clan but none the less authentic for that.

'The McTudor thermos, eh Basil?' he asked the dog, who glared back reproachfully.

The punch had been simmering since before Jazz Trethewey's arrival and was maturing more or less to his satisfaction. From time to time he added a pinch of ginger, cinammon, nutmeg or dried wattle but he did so very judiciously for he knew from a lifetime's experience that whereas you could always add to this sort of mixture you could never subtract.

It was interesting that Jazz Trethewey had been so patronizing about the idea. Ashley, or whoever had sent the last e-mail, suggested that Jazz along with her friend the bearded axeman, had monopolized the spoils of this competition in recent years. The way she was talking you would have thought she'd have nothing whatever to do with it. On the other hand Tudor guessed that her *amour propre* would be damaged if she were ever to come anywhere except top where wine was concerned – even adulterated plonk. He would soon see.

He tried to cast his mind back to university days and to remember if he and Ashley had done mulled wine. It had been a beer culture as far as he could recall. Maybe some college clubs or tutors had provided hot grog in the bleak midwinter but mixing such drinks wasn't on the undergraduate syllabus – even the extra-mural one. The college had a cellar of which legends are forged but it was a privilege confined to the senior common room. Dons only. He seemed to remember that Miranda had done champagne. That had been part of their problem. Miranda liked champagne and MG sports cars with gramophones. Neither Tudor nor Ashley could do much more than beer and bicycles. Miranda would condescend to both but she made no secret of the fact that doing so was slumming.

He sipped the brew, puckered his lips and brow thoughtfully. This was as good as it was going to get. He wondered if the concoction would have met with Ashley's approval and then, failing to find an answer to the question, moved with alarming rapidity on to asking himself whether he cared. On balance he decided that he didn't much. Concern for his old friend had given way to irritation. In other words he believed that Ashley was still alive, had disappeared on purpose and was playing silly buggers. This was not a matter of proof but of instinct. Disconcertingly he found that all his youthful beliefs about head being more reliable than heart were proving increasingly suspect. Miranda? Ashley? Mulled wine? Being fond of people or things, let alone falling in love with them, seemed natural and right in youth. Now, in middle age, it was becoming clear that it was a dangerous indulgence. Forensic intelligence was all. Feelings were folly.

It was time to decant. Tudor found a battered ladle and transferred the mull from saucepan to thermos allowing a small proportion to escape down his throat. Not bad.

He decided to check his e-mail one more time before leaving for the competition. He had no messages which, of course, meant nothing, but still left him feeling unreasonably disappointed. The e-mail messages were his only contact, real or imaginary, with his friend and host. He still couldn't be sure whether or not the communications were from Ashley but they had to be from someone and they were all he had to work with. It wasn't much but without these few words from space that was all he had: space. Ashley Carpenter had disappeared into it and was communicating from it. Everything was emptiness. Tudor was reminded of the unfinished Sherlock Holmes case concerning Mr James Phillimore 'who stepping back into his own house to get his umbrella was never more seen in this world'. And then there was the cutter *Alicia* 'which sailed one spring morning into a small patch of mist from which she never again emerged; nor was anything further ever heard of herself and her crew'. Tudor didn't want Ashley to turn into James Phillimore or the crew of the *Alicia*.

There was a half-pint or so of hot wine left after he had filled the thermos so Tudor decanted it into a half-pint mug decorated with the college crest – gum tree, wombat and parakeet above the legend *Mens sana in corpore sano*. The slogan was the target of feminist revisionists without the benefit of a classical education who considered it elitist and sexist. They wanted something in a native language such as Pitjontjajora, or at least the addition of the words 'and womens' after 'mens'. Of this, however, Tudor Cornwall knew as yet nothing. He was after all only a Visiting Fellow.

'I think a drink is called for, don't you, Basil?' said Tudor, already the worse for a half bottle of Bee's Knees and a slurp or so of the Ashley mull. Not that he was drunk or even on the way there. He was abstemious by inclination and habit but could hold his own and keep his head if and when it came to hard liquor. This wasn't often but it happened. That was in the nature of academic life and of criminal studies.

He drank the brew thoughtfully, the pungency penetrating his sinuses like Friar's Balsam. It had a distinctively Antipodean flavour which he found difficult to put into words. Was it a winner? He couldn't say but he felt it might be in with a shout.

'Good grief, Basil,' he said, out loud, 'I'm in danger of taking this thing seriously. There must be something wrong. It's a competition to find out who's produced the best mulled wine, for God's sake. I have better things to worry about than that, surely to God.'

The dog looked at him muttishly but said nothing. Tudor half-believed he would speak, an aberration he was not going to attribute to his booze intake but rather to the increasingly surreal state of mind induced by Ashley's disappearance and his new surroundings and acquaintances. He did feel as if he was a character in a shaggy dog story. After all, here he was speaking to his canine companion as if he were a human being. This way madness lay.

He pushed away the barely touched mug and stood up. This vinous competition was an ordeal which had to be faced, though he hardly knew now why he had been inveigled into taking part. He was, he realized, seriously contemplating the possibility of packing his bags, folding his tent and heading off home to the security of his office and supporting staff at the University of Wessex. That was a decision he would postpone until after this absurd blind tasting.

He wondered who would be there? Dame Edith, he presumed. Brad Davey, Jazz Trethewey, Tasman Penhaligon. They seemed to be the only resident fellows apart from Ashley. Did Lorraine Montagu enjoy the status of Fellow in her capacity as College Secretary. Sammy the Sikh would be acting as a sort of master-of-ceremonies but would surely not be entitled to a vote. The student body would presumably not be represented, not even by the balefully ubiquitous Elizabeth Burney. Was she the college tart or the college thief, or either or both? Had Ashley harassed her? Had she led him on? She was hiding something – that much was obvious – but was she concealing Ashley and if so was she doing so with his connivance or against his will? And if the latter, could she be doing so alone? It seemed impossible. In which case she must have accomplices.

He picked up his thermos in its vivid tartan livery and headed towards the door.

'Be a good boy, Basil,' he said. 'See you soon.'

Were the names he had just run through the suspects in this case, he wondered, as he locked the door and dog behind him. But what case? The case of the vanishing professor? Nobody but him seemed to regard the matter in that light. Was that in itself suspicious? If Tudor had gone absent without leave from the Department of Criminal Studies at Wessex, there would have been a speedy hue and cry. Wouldn't there? Would the Vice-Chancellor have called in the police, or decided that to do so might invite scandal? Would he and his colleagues assume that

Tudor was going through some sort of mid-life crisis and needed time and space to sort himself out? Or that he was conducting some illicit sexual liaison which he did not want discovered or even speculated about?

Put yourself in *their* position. That was what he was always telling his students. What would you have done if you were Crippen? How would you have reacted if you were the Wests in Gloucester? What would a murderer do in these circumstances? How would a victim react?

Easier said than done, he thought, ruefully. There were so few facts to go on. No body, dead or alive. Only these arch and cryptic messages on the screen of his lap-top.

He began to walk downstairs, cradling his precious flask and wondering if it held more than mulled wine. Was there a dark secret in the e-mail prescription? Was there a cryptic clue in the messages from space? Was Basil the dog that failed to bark in the dark? Was Ashley missing presumed dead, or waving not drowning? Was he going mad? Was that the intention? And if so, whose?

It was dark in the courtyard. In the distance he could hear the coo-ee of some strange foreign bird of the night. And was that the sawing of cicadas in the long grass? A thin sliver of moonlight silhouetted the mountain and the omnivorous wilderness which engulfed the countryside beyond the city boundary.

Tudor shivered. He felt a long way from home, assailed by doubt, foreignness.

'Rich cocoa,' said a voice from the cloister, 'dark chocolate, cherries, plums and toasty cedary oak. And that's just the nose. I'm sure you have a nose for such smells, Professor.'

It was Jazz Trethewey.

'And as for the palate,' she continued, 'more of the same but blueberries, mulberries, crunchy cassis, blond tobacco and cedary oak.'

'I'm sorry,' said Tudor, screwing his eyes in the direction of the voice, 'What are you talking about?'

'The Bee's Knees,' said the Professor of Wine, 'I looked up the tasting notes. You'd never have identified all those tastes and smells. But you might have got the colour. Full bodied, full blooded, sparkling red.'

'I'd never have guessed,' he said, as she fell in alongside him.

'And eat with Eggs Benedict, smoked salmon and asparagus omelette, patés, blue and white Castello cheese, soft curd and hard cheeses, antipasto, Yum Cha and, of course, blackberry pie!'

'Quite a choice.'

'Mmm,' the professor agreed. 'And serve chilled at around ten degrees celsius. It's a wine best served cold. Like revenge.'

CHAPTER FOURTEEN

The Bob Hawke room already felt familiar, though this evening's arrangements did not. A long table was set with a white cloth on which, at regular intervals, there sat small bunsen burners under trivets surmounted by copper tureens. They looked like a group of smart fondue kits gussied up to convey an impression of old-world senior common room antiquity and gravitas. The paradox was that this was achieved with more conviction than would have been managed in the real old world itself. Doctor Cornwall was impressed, not for the first time, by the way in which imitation outshone reality. Modern Oxford or Cambridge would have been all polystyrene, plastic and chrome. For the true patina of dusty leather and ancient mahogany you really needed the ivory towers of American or Australasian academe.

Sammy took Tudor's thermos with the fastidious disdain of a doctor accepting a urine sample.

'I'll allocate your entry a number,' he said, 'but I'll be the only bloke who knows what the number is. Everyone who tastes, tastes blind.' He then handed over a voting form and a pencil.

'First past the post,' he said. 'X marks the spot. Biggest number of x's wins.'

'And in the event of a tie?' asked Tudor.

'Then there's a taste-off,' said Sammy. 'One-on-one. Sort of like a penalty-shoot-out.'

Not really, he thought, but what did it matter? Taste one mulled wine and you'd tasted the lot. They were in the middle of a serious missing-person's crisis and they were supposed to become exercised over a comparative tasting of warmed spicy alcohol. In the divine order of things, the relative taste of different hot drinks rated low.

'Well, Doctor Cornwall,' said Dame Edith, fussily patting the creases out of the tablecloth. 'We do seem to be entering into the spirit of the occasion. I wish all our Visiting Fellows were so eager to assimilate and come to terms with our little ways. It makes life so much easier. I don't believe we've ever had a visitor before who's concocted their own mull, especially after such a short time in college.'

'I'm sure Doctor Cornwall is going to be a great asset,' said Jazz Trethewey. 'He's showing all the signs of being an assimilator.' She smiled conspiratorially. 'I'm afraid some of your fellow countrymen can seem more than a shade patronizing. Even in my discipline. I must say that it's a little hard to take when a Professor of Wine from Perfidious Albion starts laying down the law on vintages or *terroir* when all his own country has produced is elderflower or dandelion and burdock.'

'Oh I don't know.' Doctor Cornwall felt obliged to defend his countrymen's wine industry. 'There are one or two quite decent whites in the south of England and I believe they're doing well with pinot noir in North Cornwall.'

'Piss and wind,' said the bearded Tasman Penhaligon, who had entered left with his tartan thermos. 'Northern hemisphere wines are like northern hemisphere rugby football.'

'Doctor Penhaligon used to play open-side wing-forward for Tasmania B. He still turns out for the state veterans.' This was Brad Davey attempting, somewhat ineffectually, to be emollient. He, too, had a regulation tartan thermos which he handed over to the hard-working Sammy with an ingratiating leer. 'That should blow the bows off your sneakers, Sam,' he said.

'No alcoholic additives allowed, Brad,' said Sammy, 'The rules say instant disqualification for anyone submitting a mixture of more than thirteen per cent proof.'

'How does anyone know?' asked Tudor, mildly.

'I run a cool random drug check,' said Sammy, disappearing behind a gold and black chinoiserie screen with an armful of thermoses to which he had attached sticky yellow tabs with numbers on them. Tudor supposed he knew what he was doing. It seemed rather haphazard to him and he had no serious expectation of fair play. Whether the result depended on financial bribery or college politics he could not guess, but he did not for a moment suppose that the best man or woman would win.

'We're just waiting for Lorraine,' said the Dame, beaming round the assembled company as Sammy re-emerged and started to pour the contents of the various thermoses into the waiting tureens. Each one had a ladle by the side. The drill seemed to be that you ladled a small quantity into your individual pewter tankard, sniffed, tasted and spat, if so inclined, in to the senior common room spittoon in the middle of the room. Tudor sensed that most of them would swallow rather than spit.

'Lorraine's late for everything,' said Jazz Trethewey in an aside intended only for him, 'and recently she's been later than usual. She's not been herself these last few days. Even when she is herself she's not entirely up to speed. I'm afraid your friend Professor Carpenter has not been treating her in a gentlemanly manner.'

Tudor arched an eyebrow.

'Care to elaborate?' he said.

'Later, maybe,' replied the Professor of Oenology. 'Ah, here she is! Not in good order I'm afraid.'

This was true. The College Secretary seemed dishevelled. Her eyes had the pink, puffy appearance of someone who had been crying, though, thought Tudor, pragmatically, it might just as well have been hay fever or a heavy cold. As he was constantly telling his classes, the one thing you shouldn't do with a conclusion was to jump to it. Conclusions were there to be arrived at methodically, slowly, after all considerations had been taken into account. For that reason, if no other, he did not allow himself to assume that Lorraine Montagu had recently been in tears.

'Ah, Lorraine,' cried Dame Edith, with a heavy hint of irony, 'how good of you to come!'

'I'm sorry I'm late,' said Lorraine, handing her thermos to Sammy who gave her what looked to Tudor like a particularly sympathetic smile. 'I got held up.'

'How remiss of you,' said Dame Edith. 'However your being held up hasn't held *us* up unduly,' and she gave a dry, donnish cackle, as if she had cracked a particularly clever joke which the rest of the group were too unintelligent or ill-educated to understand.

'So!' The Dame clapped her hands together and rubbed them with a positive glow of self-satisfaction. 'Now that we are all assembled once more for this, one of our most enjoyable St Petroc's traditions . . .'

'Tradition my arse,' hissed Jazz Trethewey into Tudor's right ear. 'She invented the thing just five years ago. It's just a bad habit she's got us into.'

'Traditions,' repeated the Principal, who had noticed Professor Trethewey whispering to the Visiting Fellow and assumed that the whisper was not just a sweet nothing (sweet nothings being a completely unknown quantity as far as either of them were concerned). She had not been able to hear what was said, but could see from the scepticism on Trethewey's face and the amusement on Cornwall's that whatever had been said was evidence of bad attitude.

She then paused and stared in order to show that she had noticed the subversion and was determined to display her authority. 'In the world of wine it is said that only rot is noble.' Here she cackled another note of impenetrable superiority. 'But in the world of St Petroc's we not only talk no rot but also believe in the nobility of tradition.'

Cornwall winced. The old bird was becoming severely encumbered by the exuberance of her verbosity. He had always understood that her countrymen were remarkable for their plain-speaking and was surprised.

Dame Edith seemed surprised by this sudden flight as well and coughed as she collected herself.

'I'm sorry to have to record the absence, for the first time in several years, of our distinguished member, Professor Ashley Carpenter. However, as you know, Professor Carpenter has taken an unscheduled leave of absence. This will I trust be brief, though I should record with sorrow that Ashley has not sent me a formal apology which isn't like him. He's usually very correct about such matters.'

A sudden sob punctuated this section of the Principal's speech, causing everyone to turn to Lorraine Montagu who was obviously the culprit and was now holding a handkerchief to her mouth and pretending that she was not distressed but just had a nasty cough. Maybe she had, thought Cornwall, engaging brain as dispassionately as he could. It would be consistent with the puffy eyes. Maybe she was allergic to something. Dame Edith's oratory perhaps. He wouldn't blame her.

'It's a great pleasure that our temporary loss of Professor Carpenter has been alleviated by our gain – also temporary alas – of his friend and colleague, Doctor Tudor Cornwall, Reader in Criminal Studies at the University of Wessex, England. In fact I'm delighted to be able to tell you that even though he has hardly got over his jet-lag our Visiting Fellow has generously and inventively concocted an entry of his own to compete with the college's best. Bravo, Doctor Cornwall, and may the best mull win.'

Cornwall acknowledged this with a smile and a gentle inclination of his head. Everyone except the green axeman, who frowned aggressively, and Lorraine Montagu who still had her handkerchief held to her mouth, smiled back.

'And so. Sammy has explained the rules,' said the Dame. 'Let us now imbibe, ingest, expectorate if you must, cogitate, deliberate and finally determine which recipe it shall be that is St Petroc's mulled wine of the year.' And she raised her still empty pewter goblet in a sort of general gesture of goodwill which indicated that they were no longer under starter's orders but were well and truly off.

There was now a sort of corporate lunge towards the various tureens which were giving off a collective aroma of fuggy, figgy wine overlaid with a general reek of clove, cinnamon, orange peel and, for all Cornwall knew, bats' wings, newts' livers and, in deference to Dame Edith's speciality, some exotic bits and pieces of echidna. Quills perhaps. How unfortunate, if picturesque, to die because of a miniature porcupine needle stuck in one's throat.

Suddenly this was a terrible thought to have had.

One of the company shrieked.

The sound was agonized, threatened, strangulated.

Lorraine Montagu had dropped her pewter goblet, splashing warm red wine all over crisp cream blouse. Her hands were tearing at her throat as if she needed to unscrew her head to pull out the monster which was throttling her, starving her of breath, stifling the life out of her, as they watched impotently, enthralled, disbelieving and aghast.

For a second they stood transfixed, their silence sliced through by the agonized woman's cries of anguish. Then there was a hubbub of confused concern. 'Water!' shouted someone; 'Ice!' screamed another. 'Loosen her collar!' 'Lie her down!' 'Turn her over!' 'For Christ's sake, do something!'

Cornwall, whose experience in such matters was almost entirely academic, was quicker than most, catching her in his arms as she fell, hands still scrabbling at her neck, face puce, eyes starting with pain and fear. But he was too late to do anything but support her weight and offer a comfort which was cold indeed. Before anyone could minister ice, water, or even a last rite, Lorraine Montagu gave a final scream that faded away into the glühwein atmosphere like the Last Post on a foggy night on the Somme, twitched convulsively and then went horribly, definitively and unequivocally, limp.

Tudor, very gently, cradled her, laid her down to rest, and looked up at the horrified wine tasters.

For a few moments no one spoke. The careless bonhomie of the occasion was shattered, each individual too shocked to say anything and quite unable to find words to match the horror of the happening.

Then, inevitably, the Dame took what for want of a better word, one might have described as 'charge'.

'Sammy,' she said with a flatness, even the suspicion of a quaver, quite at odds with her earlier bombast, 'Phone for Dr Simkiss!'

'It's a bit late for Dr Simkiss,' said Tudor Cornwall. 'Phone for him by all means but once you've done that, Sammy, I think you'd better call the police.'

CHAPTER FIFTEEN

Doctor Simkiss and the police performed their tasks with customary efficiency.

Simkiss was the college doctor, sour in manner and cadaverous in appearance. His duties consisted merely of confirming that the wretched woman was dead. As to the cause of death he was not to be drawn beyond the obvious conclusion that she seemed to have suffered some form of asphyxia. Cornwall's private observation was that Dr Simkiss hadn't a clue. He was reminded of the crisp Randolph Churchill aphorism concerning his father Sir Winston, in extreme old age. Sir Winston's doctor, almost as decrepit as Churchill himself, was Lord Moran. Randolph regarded Moran as wholly incompetent and issued an instruction to his father's staff which said, 'If my father is taken ill, phone Lord Moran and get him to send for a doctor.'

Watching Dr Simkiss feel forlornly for poor Lorraine's non-existent pulse Tudor felt like telling him to send for a proper doctor. He would certainly not be consulting Dr Simkiss if he fell ill. On the other hand there was nothing Simkiss could do beyond remarking with a melancholy air, 'There'll have to be a post-mortem examination.'

The police performance was more encouraging. Tudor was pleased though surprised to discover that one of the investigating officers was Karen White, the young police constable who had been assigned to the disappearance of Ashley Carpenter. Tudor did not hold her scepticism against her although he would have been dismayed if she was the only police person on the case.This time, however, she was not alone. Her companion was a fresh-faced man who, Tudor, guessed, was older than he looked which to his increasingly jaded eye was about twenty-eight going on twelve.

'I'm really pleased to meet you, Dr Cornwall,' he said. 'I couldn't believe it when Karen told me you were visiting St Petroc's. I'm a fan. I guess I must have read most everything you've ever written. That essay of yours on the Bodkin Adams case in last month's *Australian Crime Quarterly* was a masterpiece.'

'Thank you,' said Cornwall. He hadn't realized the piece had been reprinted in Australia and couldn't recollect receiving a fee. He must have a word with his agent.

'The parallels with Shipman are fascinating. I wish we still had crime reporters like Percy Hoskins. They don't seem to make them like him any more.'

'No,' Cornwall agreed, though it was not the sort of verdict usually delivered by one so young. 'I'm sorry. What did you say your name was?'

'Greg,' said the not-so-young man. 'Greg Sanders. Chief Inspector, Hobart CID. I couldn't believe my luck when the call came in just now. I'd no idea I'd be getting to meet you so soon.'

'Well,' Cornwall was unsurprised by the apparent callousness though he found its expression somewhat startling. 'I could have wished that we were meeting under slightly more propitious circumstances.'

'Oh.' Greg grinned ruefully and shook his head. 'I see what you mean. Yeah. I'm sorry. Listen, I'm going to have to take statements but maybe you and I could meet up for a beer or a drop of red when you have a spare moment.'

Tudor wished yet again, that he didn't so often find himself sounding like the archetypal pompous Pom. Only a certain sort of Englishman would use a phrase like 'slightly more propitious circumstances' and he wasn't, he kept telling himself, at all that sort of starchy, prune-up-the-bum, sort of English person. Far from it. He prided himself on his informality, his contempt for convention, lack of respect for pettifogging bureaucracy.

'Sure,' he said, trying to strike the right note, 'but don't let me interfere with your job.'

Greg flushed and Tudor realized that he had sounded supercilious. Dammit, he thought. Ease up!

The police job at this point consisted of taking statements. In fact, Cornwall realized, there was no obligation for them to do so and correspondingly the witnesses had no duty to assist them. On the face of it there was no need for a police presence. If poor Lorraine had choked to death on a fish-bone or, as he had fancifully conjectured – to his present mortification – an echidna quill, it would never have occurred to anyone that the police should become involved. Sudden death need not concern the police unless there was a crime involved. Oh, all right, he agreed with himself, road accidents. But road accidents always carried the chance of dangerous or careless driving, or drugs, or drink. Choking to death for reason or reasons unknown had no criminal connotations unless the victim was throttled by another party or was poisoned. Had Lorraine Montagu been poisoned? She had seemed unwell on arrival. Correction, she had seemed upset. That very public sob of hers could not have been an early warning of her fatal spasm. Or could it? If she had not died from natural causes, poison would have to be considered. If it was poison then the killer would have had to cause her to ingest some substance which only she would swallow. That ruled out the mulled wines because the rules of the competition were, of course, that everyone should have a taste of everything. There was no way any poisoner could have introduced something lethal into Lorraine's sample without putting it in everyone else's drink. Unless Sammy had practised some inventive sleight of hand. Tudor remembered the sympathetic almost conspiratorial smile Sammy had given the College Secretary when she arrived late. That could not have been the smile of a murderer for his victim, surely? Effective bluff but not plausible.

These various thoughts and conjectures hurried through Cornwall's brain in a matter of nano-seconds. They were, perhaps necessarily, inconclusive, but he realized, with a shock, that he was not seriously considering that Lorraine Montagu had died from natural causes. His suspicion was instinctive. No more than a hunch. But his hunches frequently proved correct. Too often for comfort, certainly too often to be ignored. 'The role of intuition in the detection of crime' was one of his most contentious lectures. Conventional wisdom, especially that of police procedural, ruled that there was no such thing as intuition in the armoury of the modern detective. Everything was scientific. DNA ruled. The catching of criminals and the detecting of crime were nowadays regarded as exact sciences. Cornwall recognized the place of science in criminal investigation but despite that he regarded detection as an art with all the inexplicable mysteries that such a definition involved.

Sammy had placed a sheet over the corpse with almost indecent haste and soon after the arrival of the police, the body was stretchered away by men in white coats, destined for the morgue and then for forensic pathology. Cornwall remained squeamish about pathology, did not even enjoy reading about it, especially when its gory details were rendered into fictional entertainment. He could not bring himself to read the work of his namesake Patricia, brilliant though he admitted it to be.

Detective Chief Inspector Sanders and Police Constable White were taking statements next door in the college's Mining Library. This was a room devoted entirely to books on mining in Tasmania and elsewhere based on the Kitto Bequest, a collection of books and papers left to St Petroc's by Sir Ebenezer Kitto, the

Cornish-born engineer and philanthropist who had first discovered the rich veins of copper behind the Wurlitzer Mountain on which the state's once prosperous economy had originally been based. It was reputed to be the best such collection outside the Camborne School of Mines.

DCI Sanders asked them all to stay where they were, to leave everything as it was and not to discuss what had happened. None of this was difficult. Cornwall certainly didn't feel like conversation, much less mulled wine, and was content to sit in glummish contemplation, a mood which was obviously infectious. Gradually each person was called for interview and did not return. Eventually only he was left until finally, at about 9 p.m., he too was summoned.

'I'd buy you that drink now,' said Sanders, 'but we have rules about alcohol on duty. Certainly rules about alcohol in uniform.' He himself was in blue jeans, an open neck check shirt and a bomber jacket. WPC White, however, was in regulation policewoman's kit much like that worn by the British organization on which the Tasmanian police force was based.

Cornwall nodded. 'Of course,' he said.

'I was a student here myself,' said Sanders, 'Long before Dame Edith, let alone the other Fellows. The principal in my day was Ebenezer Kitto's grandson, Bevil.'

'Ah.' There seemed no very obvious response.

'I studied Classics,' Sanders continued. 'I used to write Latin verses for Bevil Kitto's tutorials. He was an Ovid freak.'

'Unusual background for a copper.'

'People say I'm an unusual cop. But Hobart's an unusual town; Tasmania's an unusual state; and St Petroc's is definitely an unusual college. So I guess in a way I'm depressingly conventional.' He paused. 'Doctor Cornwall, may I ask you a question?'

'That's what I'm here for.'

'Doctor Cornwall, can you tell me why you're here?'

'I think that's an Everest sort of a question.'

'Pardon me?'

'You know. When Mallory was asked why he wanted to climb Mount Everest. Or maybe it was Irving. I forget. They both died. When whichever one it was, was asked why he had this ambition to climb the world's tallest mountain he said it was because it was there. "Why do you want to climb Mount Everest?" "Because it's there." Why am I Visiting Fellow at St Petroc's College in the University of Tasmania? Because the opportunity presented itself. Like Everest for the climber. I could have said "yes" or I could have said "no". On balance, I'm a person who normally says "yes". I enjoy challenge. I like the unknown.'

'But we're not exactly in the mainstream here. You have an international reputation. You could have been a Visiting Fellow anywhere you wanted. Harvard. Yale. Adelaide.'

'You're too kind, but you under-rate yourself. I agree that Tasmania's a small state and it's a long way from where I live. But Professor Carpenter has a considerable reputation himself. He's built up a lively department. And there's a lot of interesting raw material from the convict past to the criminal present.'

Chief Inspector Sanders gave a wry smile. 'I agree,' he said, 'Our criminal record's impressive. Always has been. Isn't that correct, Karen?'

The police constable, sitting at a table to his left, pencil poised over a standard-issue loose-leaf notebook, smiled and nodded. She gave the impression of being slightly overawed by her senior.

'Professor Carpenter,' said Sanders. 'I've heard him lecture but I wouldn't say I know him. You, on the other hand, are an old and close friend.'

'Old,' agreed Tudor, 'and once close. But it's difficult to maintain a very close relationship when you're based at opposite ends of the earth. We've remained in touch though.'

'He in Tasmania, you in Wessex.'

'Yes. But we meet up at international conferences. They're crucial to academic life these days. We see each other at least twice a year. At Harvard once. Adelaide even.'

Sanders smiled. '*Touché*,' he said, 'And it was Professor Carpenter who asked you to spend a semester here as Visiting Fellow?'

'Yes.'

'And why was that exactly?'

Cornwall found himself becoming irritated but curbed his inclination to snap. The man was only doing his job, albeit in a strangely circuitous maner. Cornwall knew he should find this round-about approach attractive and realized that the only reason he was annoyed was that he was the one who seemed to be under the magnifying glass. Usually it was the other way round.

'That's another Everest question,' he said.

'He asked you because you were there?' Sanders smiled innocently.

'In a manner of speaking, yes. I mean St Petroc's has a Visiting Fellow programme. Ashley thought I might have something to contribute. He knows I don't have any family ties or commitments, so that provided I could square it with my Vice-Chancellor and colleagues I'd have no problem taking a sort of sabbatical. And it would give the two of us a chance to compare notes and to catch up.'

'And now that you've arrived he's not here to welcome you?'

'No.'

'And that strikes you as curious?'

'Yes.'

'Me too.' Sanders looked at the fingernails on his right hand as if they were about to yield up some remarkable secret, then flashed another boyish grin.

'But none of your new colleagues seem concerned by his absence?'

'Not a lot, no.'

'I find that curious too,' said Sanders. 'How about you, Dr Cornwall?'

'Well, yes. Me too. But I'm not sure what any of this has to do with Lorraine Montagu's death.'

'Nor am I,' said the Chief Inspector, 'but like you I'm curious. I'd like to talk more. Maybe when we have the results of the post-mortem.'

He frowned, cleared his throat and changed gear. His new voice indicated that he had moved out of official mode and into something more conversational and off-the-record, though Cornwall sensed that this was one policeman who was never wholly off-duty.

'Tell me more about the Bodkin Adams case,' he said. 'I'm fascinated to know what makes some doctors kill.'

CHAPTER SIXTEEN

Tudor was tired by the time he returned to his quarters but Basil was frisky and, he assumed, in need of a pee.

'Oh all right, Bazza,' he said, 'walkies.' And Basil jumped up at him appreciatively, wagging his tail and whimpering with apparent pleasure.

'You're a fickle fellow, aren't you?' This was Ashley's dog, he had to remind himself, and dogs were supposed to be loyal and, as far as humans were concerned, more or less monogamous. 'I am his master's dog at Kew. Pray tell me sir, whose dog are you?' he recited, at the excited animal which cocked his head and looked at him with the nearest approach to a quizzical manner that a dog could muster. Why would Ashley abandon him? Or had Basil escaped? And if he had escaped, then what or who from?

'I wish you could say something intelligent,' Tudor said and couldn't help smiling when the dog gave him the sort of glance which managed to imply that if it was intelligence that was in question he could give as good as he got. Speech, he seemed to be suggesting, was a much over-rated commodity.

Outside, the sky was clear and the air bracing. Tudor identified Ursa Major, Orion and the Southern Cross, which was more or less the extent of his stellar capability. The Milky Way looked pretenaturally, well, milky. The atmosphere was less polluted down here but they were right under a hole in the ozone layer. Win some, lose some. Cornwall didn't spend a lot of time contemplating the future of the planet or of mankind. The study of crime was essentially the study of individuals, not Big Bangs. Therein, for Tudor, lay its fascination.

They were just walking under the creeper-covered archway that led into the main quadrangle when Basil who had been lolloping around in a doggy fashion, sniffing at the odd bush, cocking his leg against trees and walls and generally doing the blokeish things one expected from a blue-heeler cross, suddenly stopped in his tracks and started to growl at a recessed doorway. Cornwall sensed the hackles rise on the dog's back and felt a corresponding tickle in his own spine. The moon had gone behind a cloud and it was momentarily quite dark. Then the cloud passed, the dog growled with what sounded like real menace and a shaft of light illuminated the face of a figure in the doorway. Elizabeth Burney.

'Hi, Doctor Cornwall,' she called in a coquettish stage whisper. 'Are you looking after Professor Carpenter's Basil? Cool. Hi, Basil!'

Basil stopped growling, went up to her, tail wagging and allowed his head to be patted.

'That's real cute,' she said. 'Professor Carpenter must be lost without him.'

'With or without him Professor Carpenter seems to be hopelessly lost. What are you doing? Surely you should be in bed asleep? Or burning some midnight oil. Don't students have essay crises any more?'

'I couldn't sleep,' she said. 'What's been going on? I saw Dr Simkiss and a police car and an ambulance. Someone was taken away on a stretcher. I'm frightened. What's going on?'

'It's nothing whatever to do with you,' said Cornwall, not believing a word he said. 'And if I were you I'd cut along to bed and get a good night's sleep.'

'I'm frightened,' she said, 'I really am. I don't like to be on my own. I don't feel safe. First Professor Carpenter vanishes and now this.'

'Now nothing,' he said firmly, not believing what she said any more than he believed what he said himself. Elizabeth Burney wasn't lurking in dark doorways late at night because she was frightened. If she was really frightened she'd be tucked up in bed with a good book and a hot drink. Or, given her reputation, with a protective male for company and safe-keeping.

'As soon as I've given Basil his exercise I'm going to bed myself and I strongly advise you to do the same.'

'Can I come too?' she giggled sexily, not sounding even remotely fearful. And before he could protect himself she had flung her arms round him and was hugging him in a tight embrace.

Seconds after she had made this move there was a bellow from the shadows and Cornwall found himself transfixed in the glare of a bright spotlight. Basil gave out an angry yelp and bounded towards the source of light, clearly intent on defending his temporary master and the importunate college tart. Cornwall realized with a sinking heart that he had been set up.

'Christ! You bastard mutt! Get that dog off me, Cornwall!'

Basil was clearly doing a good job. Tudor thought he recognized the rambunctious voice of Tasman Penhaligon, the green axeman, and was not displeased to register the fact that he appeared to be experiencing pain.

'He's not my dog, Penhaligon,' he called, 'I've no control over him whatever.'

'Bastard!' hissed Penhaligon, 'He's bloody lucky not to be decapitated. You British shit! I'll have your arse for after, guts for garters, brains for . . .'

'Sounds as if Basil has your ankles for hors-d'oeuvres,' said Cornwall. 'Why don't you advance and be recognized and explain what the hell you're playing at?'

Attack best form of defence; old British maxim. It seemed to work. Tasman Penhaligon lurched out of the shadows with the dog appended to his lower left leg like some grizzling, wriggling growth. Basil was clearly not going to let go in a hurry and it must have been a relief to Penhaligon to be wearing thick sensible trousers. He held a torch in his left hand and, true to form, a hatchet in his right.

'What in heaven's name are you doing with that axe?' asked Cornwall, incredulous.

Penhaligon did not seem abashed but shook his leg furiously in a vain attempt to dislodge the limpet-like hound. Basil hung on.

'Get that dog off!' Penhaligon was growling himself.

'Drop, Basil! There's a good boy.' It was the girl who spoke. Basil, with Penhaligon's leg still in his jaws, gave a valedictory flurry of shaking, making a defiant 'wirra-wirra-wirra' noise and then backed off still glowering up at his quarry. Elizabeth Burney obviously had a way with dogs, or at least with Basil. Even in this curious and possibly tight spot Cornwall was impressed and also intrigued.

There was a moment's silence during which the collective collection of wits was almost tangible.

Then all three spoke at once.

Cornwall said, 'What on earth are you doing wandering around college with that axe?'

Penhaligon said, 'What's your game, pommy son-of-a-bitch bastard?'

Elizabeth Burney said, 'I'm going to bed.'

There was another pause and then Penhaligon said, 'I'm duty tutor which means I'm responsible for the college's safety and security, which means I do the rounds to make sure everything's properly safe and secure. Like in bed and asleep.'

'With a bloody axe?'

'I'm a bloody axeman. If I find someone here who shouldn't be here I have to have a means of defence. We have a crime situation here in Tasmania. These guys carry knives and guns and believe me they aren't afraid to use them. I have a right and you're effing lucky not to feel the sharp end of it. Hadn't been for the girl here there's no telling what could have happened to you. And you'd have no one to blame but you. Horse-shit!'

He had bent down to rub the leg from which Basil had just become detached and realized that his hand – the one holding the torch – was covered in blood.

'That rabid beast of yours has drawn bloody blood.' He aimed a kick at Basil which the dog easily evaded.

'You shouldn't be out and about with a weapon like that.'

'Who the eff says? I'm on college property. The Principal knows I'm armed. Who the hell are you to tell me what I should be doing?'

'You seem to forget that I'm a Reader in Criminal Studies. As such I'm required to know the law. If you hurt someone with that axe it's anything from assault to grievous bodily harm. If you kill someone, it's murder.'

'Wanker! It's self-defence. And you may be a Reader in Criminal Studies but you're just like your friend Carpenter. Criminal studies, my arse! You're only here for the sex. Well, those days have changed, my friend. We take a strong line on sexual harassment here in Tasmania. You may think we're a load of primitive savages descended from people you transported out here a hundred and more years ago but I'm here to tell you that when it comes to civilized behaviour you're the primitive savages and we're the ones with the Nobel Prize for ethics and female emancipation. So what exactly were you doing trying to rape one of St Petroc's girls in the middle of the night?'

'He wasn't trying to rape me, Dr Penhaligon,' said Elizabeth Burney, slightly unexpectedly. 'Now I really am going to bed. Alone. And I suggest you two do the same. Also alone. Jesus! Men!'

And before either man could do anything to prevent her, she

was striding defiantly away in the direction, presumably, of her room. After a moment of hesitation, the dog followed her. Tudor thought of remonstrating but decided it would seem undignified, besides which he had no more claim on the dog than anyone else. Basil clearly had a mind of his own and he was exercising it. In any case, Basil was the least of his worries and could perfectly well be sorted out in the morning. If his real master never returned he was sure a dog of his character would have no shortage of offers. Still, it was interesting that he should have followed little Miss Burney without a murmur. She herself had made no discernible effort to suborn him. Basil had gone entirely of his own accord.

Maybe the girl just had that sort of effect on people. On animals. Maybe she was not the scheming, manipulative little vixen which Cornwall assumed she was. Perhaps she just had personal magnetism.

'That seems an entirely sensible suggestion to me,' said Cornwall. 'It's well past all our bedtimes.'

The words could not have been better calculated to annoy an already infuriated not to mention wounded Tasmanian academic with an axe in his hand. Words, however, failed the green doctor.

It was also evident that this altercation, brief though it was, and conducted throughout in histrionic stage whispers had the inevitable effect of waking one or two people up. Lights were flicking on all over the place. Curtains and blinds were being drawn and raised. At one window the stout, squat and unmistakable figure of the Principal herself could be seen blinking out into the darkness of the quadrangle.

'Is that you, Tasman? Is there any problem?' she called.

'All well, Dame Edith. Just fell over a possum trying to get into the pantry.'

Despite himself, Tudor Cornwall was impressed by Penhaligon's self-control and powers of invention.

'See me in the morning,' called the Dame imperiously, 'and

don't make such a din. Possum or no possum.'

Cornwall used this intervention to slip away quietly. He had no wish to prolong the discussion, much less to end up on the wrong end of the axeman's axe. He doubted whether even an uncouth ape like Penhaligon would have risked wounding him with what was almost certainly a well-honed blade, but he certainly wouldn't have been surprised by a blow with the blunt end.Or even just a kick or punch where it would hurt most. If he really was the duty tutor it would presumably be easy for Penhaligon to manufacture excuses.

So Tudor Cornwall returned dogless to his room with much to ponder. He would like to have slept but found it impossible, at least at first. Instead, he poured himself a stiff duty-free Famous Grouse and sipped it while he stared thoughtfully at the ceiling of his impersonal guest room and pondered the events of the last few hours wondering whether he might take the first available plane home but realizing gloomily that he would almost certainly not be allowed.

That baby-faced chief inspector would refuse him permission to leave – in the nicest possible way, of course, and making it clear that he was entirely at liberty to do as he pleased. That might have been true when there was only a disappearance to investigate but now there was a death and Doctor Cornwall was a witness.

He was experienced and alarmed enough to realize that he might also, even, absurd though it might seem, be a suspect.

CHAPTER SEVENTEEN

Tudor Cornwall was not a breakfaster. His constitution was such that he preferred to stick to liquids – sweet Indian tea with milk, followed around mid-morning by black coffee, preferably not instant – until other people's lunch. That was his breakfast. Sometimes orange juice came into the equation but not often.

At home where he lived off-campus, on his own, in a penthouse flat, overlooking the West River, this was perfectly possible. Here, in Hobart, as a guest in college, he felt obliged to at least go through the motions of conventional breakfast which was taken in Hall along with the rest of the college. This, in a ritual piece of lip-service to democracy, included students but the Fellows took their meal at High Table where they were waited on by a couple of regular maids under the beady supervision of Sammy. They ate the same food and drank the same drink as the students but they did not have to help themselves. In a perverse way this emphasized the inegality of college life far more than if, as in the old days, they had taken their breakfast in the privacy of the senior common room. Then they were merely unequal. Now they were *seen* to be unequal. Far worse.

Tudor did not want breakfast. He had gone to sleep late and slept fitfully. He had allowed himself a second scotch which he now regretted. All he wanted now was a strong mug of milky Twining's Darjeeling with two or three lumps and *The Times* crossword. What he emphatically did *not* want was Dame Edith, the Mad Axeman, the febrile *Professeuse du Vin* or even the lugubrious Brad. He did not relish the thought of tables full of young men with baseball caps turned back to front and nubile Elizabeth Burneys in over-tight vests. Nor did he fancy yoghurt, prunes, rubbery fried eggs and frazzled bacon. Not even toast and marmalade. At least, however, there would be tea.

He caught the World Service news on his ancient much loved Roberts transistor and was at once homesick yet thankful not to be home with its doleful mixture of Irish bombs, railway disasters, Manchester United victories, gales, floods and a government ban on a new magazine which was expressing a point of view with which the government did not agree and was therefore categorized as inciting people to something illegal,

Tudor was British to his fingertips and yet he despaired of the place. Even crime seemed to have gone downmarket. It was not just that nobody had butlers and libraries any longer nor that hereditary peers had been more or less expelled from the House of Lords. In fact he was ambivalent about domestic servants and the hereditary peerage and although passionate on behalf of libraries he believed in books for all. Despite all this he liked an elegance or originality in crime. He was not snobbish in the way that Dorothy L. Sayers had been, but he shared the belief of P.D. James (who had been wilfully misunderstood) that common or garden crimes committed by habitual and petty criminals were, on the whole, uninteresting. Interesting crime was crime committed by people who were not habitual criminals. On the whole this did not include the senior common rooms of even dim universities. This meant, as far as he was concerned, that common room crime was, *ipso facto*, more interesting than crime in the Crumlin Road or crime in Kinshasa. He was well aware that this attitude infuriated *soi-disant* radicals and *bien-penseurs*. This didn't bother him. Part of being a proper academic or intellectual was the ability to think in a way untrammelled by fashion. He was not so bigoted that he dismissed all politcal correctness out of hand, but he most certainly did not accept it because it was deemed correct by some mythical majority. It was his job to think the unthinkable and the trouble with his home country was that it seemed to be having increasing trouble in accommodating people like himself. It was becoming a country of over-zealous bigotry cloaked in bogus moderation. The result seemed to be increasing violence and philistinism.

The morning's World Service therefore compounded the dissatisfaction and unease left over from the events of the previous night. He nicked himself shaving which made him even tetchier, especially as he didn't notice a second cut on his neck till too late and got blood on his collar which meant discarding an otherwise pristine shirt. He also had a hole in his right sock which made him ponder the wife question as he did so often. Wives took care of socks and shirts, didn't they? If so, shouldn't he have one? No, he was too set in his ways to live with anyone again. Bad enough to have to share breakfast with his fellow Fellows. To have to share it with the same person day in, day out for the rest of his life . . . he shuddered, tightened his tie, ran his comb through his obstinate hair for a third time, dusted non-existent dandruff from his jacket shoulders and lapels and set off to face the world.

Don't be so bloody negative, he said to himself as he descended the stairs. Whistle a happy tune. One more step along the way we go.

As the result of which he entered Hall with a light tread and the suspicion of a smile on his face. No sooner had he entered the college's glorified works canteen than the first turned to lead and the second was wiped off his face before it had properly emerged. The students were all in place and as expected with the baseball caps and the vests deployed in the prescribed manner. At High Table the Principal and the Fellows were all sitting in their usual places consuming their usual breakfasts in their more or less usual way, though even a casual observer might have observed a certain tension in the air. No one spoke. The atmosphere was conveyed entirely by a stiff apprehension in the body language.

The cause of this departure from normality was sitting at one end of the High Table laying in to a plate of fried eggs and bacon. As Tudor entered he looked up, grinned as if he had not a care in the world, wiped a smudge of yolk from his upper lip with a damask SCR napkin and said, 'Tudor, my dear fellow! How good to see you!'

It was Ashley Carpenter.

The rest of High Table stared at their plates with rapt concentration. This was bogus, of course. The St Petroc Fellows were mesmerized by the meeting of the two old criminologist friends but they were determined not to be involved. They were spectators, but in order to be effective spectators they had to keep their heads down and out of the line of eye contact. Tudor recognized this. He also realized that if his old friend was halfway through his bacon and eggs he must have been at table for some little time. It looked as if everyone else had been there for a while too. Sammy was always there well before the meal began. In other words there must have been some form of confabulation. Not for the first time Tudor felt the victim of a conspiracy, but the nature of the conspiracy still eluded him.

'Ashley!' he said, and then, fatuously perhaps, but unable for the moment to think of anything more imaginative or profound, he said, 'Good to see you too.'

He wasn't sure that he meant it.

'I'm sorry,' Ashley frowned at a piece of bacon rind which was refusing to be bisected by his blunt St Petroc's knife, 'that I wasn't here to greet you. But I understand you've settled in satisfactorily.'

'Oh yes,' said Tudor, 'quite satisfactorily. Everyone has been very kind.' This is mad, he said to himself. Why are we mouthing platitudes at each other? Why are we being so polite? What is the point of these civilities?

'I'm afraid I met with a slight accident,' said Ashley. He had succeeded in cutting off the piece of bacon and put it in his mouth halfway through the sentence. 'Some sort of muscle strain. Or pull. Hamstring. Much better now thanks.' He swallowed, then took a mouthful of coffee from the mug and swallowed it rather too soon after the food to be aesthetically pleasing. Particularly at breakfast. The silent distance of the other Fellows became even more obvious. They were all clearly agog waiting for the Visiting Fellow's reaction, but they were also, just as clearly, doing a sad ostrich impression. They were so many beaks stuck in the sand while their nether portions waggled, embarassingly exposed to anyone who happened to be passing by.

'Muscle strain,' said Cornwall eventually. His voice sounded strangulated. He poured tea from the pot, added milk and sugar, stirred busily. 'Hamstring. I'm sorry I don't quite understand.'

'Nothing to understand, old boy,' said Ashley. 'Went for the usual early morning constitutional. Strained something in the leg. Had gone further than realized. Unable to walk home. Holed up in mountain hut till the leg mended, then sauntered back and here I am. Welcome to St Petroc's.'

'It's a bit late for a welcome to St Petroc's,' said Tudor, 'but it's good to see you. I'm sorry you've been in the wars. I was worried. I think we all were.'

'No worries, Dr Cornwall!' The Dame had removed her metaphorical beak from the metaphorical desert and was pushing her chair back preparatory to departure. She seemed satisfied that there was to be no unseemly row or unpleasantness, that the two old friends were going to accept Ashley Carpenter's feeble explanation for absence without leave, and that college life could continue on a more or less even keel. She dabbed at her lips with her napkin, then rolled it up tidily and threaded it into the silver ring on her side-plate. 'No worries, no trubs!' She smiled. 'Ashley's far too experienced a bushman to cause us any anxiety even if he can be a little cavalier at times.' She flashed a school-marmy frown of reproof. 'Very naughty to run off without telling us, Ashley. Especially with your friend about to descend on us. Caused us all a great deal of inconvenience.'

And she stood up and waddled away, humming tunelessly like an ancient bee.

'You could have sent a message.' Cornwall spoke quietly, privately, though he was well aware that he was being listened to by everyone else at the table. Jazz Trethewey was pretending to do the quick crossword on the back page of the *Hobart New Frontier*. The Axeman was scowling at a half-eaten kiwi fruit. Cornwall himself, shaking slightly he realized to his embarrassment, succumbed to the stress of the moment by spreading a slice of cold toast with some vile but healthy butter substitute and topped it with a thick wodge of marmalade.

'Message, old boy! I told you I was laid up in a mountain hut in the middle of nowhere. Lucky I knew it was there as a matter of fact. It's tucked in behind Hop Pickers' Gully where the college abseiling team train. Luckily they'd left behind about a hundredweight of tinned spam and beetroot so I wasn't going to starve.'

'Well I'm pleased you were able to eat,' said Cornwall, crunching toast himself, 'and I'm really sorry about the leg. But we, I, was worried. We could have come and rescued you. Air ambulance, dog and sleigh, eight wheel drive . . . whatever you have.'

His old friend regarded him levelly, appraisingly and then, as if imparting a confidence, 'Well, to be honest, old friend, I was grateful for a day or so of solitude. A wee bit of space didn't exactly come amiss.'

'But just a message to say where you were and that you were all right . . . that wouldn't have been difficult.'

'And how exactly would I have sent the good news from Hop Pickers' Gully to St Petroc's College? Native runner with cleft stick? Smoke signal? Semaphore?'

'E-mail I would assume,' said Cornwall, frostily, beginning to add that he'd been busy enough sending e-mail instructions about mulled wine when he was silenced by Ashley butting in with, 'E-mail old boy? And what makes you think the college abseiling team keep a computer in their hut?'

And when Tudor said, equally icily, 'Your laptop . . .' he was met with a glare of disbelief and the words, 'What on earth makes you think I'd take my laptop for an early morning walk up the Wurlitzer?'

It was a perfectly fair question and one which Dr Cornwall had been asking himself ever since he fielded the first of his recent messages from way out in the ether.

This was not the answer he had been expecting.

CHAPTER EIGHTEEN

Cornwall was at sea. The rest of breakfast continued in a fashion as resolutely stilted as the initial exchanges between himself and Ashley. Perhaps, he told himself, that was inevitable, given the fact that they were playing to such an attentive audience.

He remembered the British Prime Minister, 'Sunny Jim' Callaghan, blowing his re-election chances in the 1970s by responding to an almost complete breakdown of all public services and utilities in his country with the breezy dismissal, 'Crisis?! What crisis?!'

Disappearance? he said to himself. Death? Wine-tasting? No, no, he must be in dream-time. Here was his old friend and colleague scoffing an old-fashioned breakfast, cheerily chatting about a country ramble curtailed by an irksome tweak to the hamstring. Meanwhile, the college secretary, his alleged mistress, was lying dead in a down-town morgue.

Cornwall raised the matter albeit tentatively and was rebuffed.

'Not now, old boy,' said Ashley. 'Dame Edith told me but she also told me that the CID were adamant about no-speaks on the subject until further notice. Desolated, naturally, but these things happen and, well, what can one say? Would you mind passing the marmalade?'

Tudor passed the marmalade which was Frank Cooper's Oxford, complete with a coat of arms indicating that its manufacturers were suppliers of the stuff to Her Majesty the Queen.

'You and I have to talk,' said Tudor. His teeth when he said this were not exactly gritted but there was precious little space between the upper and lower sets.

'We *are* talking.' Ashley grinned wolfishly and spooned a large gob of chunky orange preserve on to his plate. 'Rather iron rations these last few days, I'm afraid. I could eat the proverbial horse.'

Tudor couldn't for the life of him see what Ashley had to be so cheerful about.

'I mean talk as in *talk*.' Tudor was still on the verge of gnashing his teeth. 'Meaningful exchange of words. There are things that need explaining.'

'Oh. If you say, so. Never apologize, never explain.'

'That was George Bernard Shaw in *Arms and the Man*,' said Tudor evenly. 'I've always thought it was arrogant rubbish. Like a lot of Shaw.'

'If you say so. We colonials don't have the advantage of your erudition. Even if we did attend one of your universities.'

'I only mean,' Tudor tried to sound placatory, 'that we have some catching up to do. I'd like to talk even if it's only about my classes. The students. The syllabus.'

Ashley crunched on his toast, brushed crumbs from his lips.

'Not a problem,' he said. 'Come to my rooms before lunch. I'm a little behind with several things but then we can catch up. Sure. Fine.'

He took a slurp of coffee, dabbed again at this lips with his napkin, and hurried out, leaving Tudor uncharacteristically slack-jawed.

The whirring of cogs in Tudor's brain was so deafening that he did not realize that Sammy was trying to attract his attention until the college servant actually tapped him on the shoulder. The room was virtually empty now. Sammy flashed very white teeth, though Tudor was not sure the smile carried any warmth or sincerity. 'Steady! Paranoia!' he found himself muttering. You could be over-suspicious in this line of work. Sometimes things actually were what they seemed. Sometimes some people were just trying to be friendly. There was no particular reason to think that Sammy was not on-side.

'I'm sorry.' Tudor smiled wearily. 'I was thinking.'

Sammy smiled more broadly, as much as to say that the condition was endemic to college life and responsible for many of the place's misfortunes.

'The police, sir,' said Sammy, in a stage whisper delivered into Tudor's right ear at point-blank range. 'The Chief Inspector is in the porter's lodge.' There was no porter's lodge as such, there being no college porter and no lodge either. It was a conceit of the Dame's. What Sammy meant was that the Chief Inspector was at the front gate.

When Tudor got to the front gate he found DCI Sanders looking even more absurdly young than he had done the night before. He had obviously slept better than Tudor and had less on his mind. He was wearing jeans and a leather bomber jacket.

'Do you remember,' he began without preamble, 'Violet Kray, the twins' mum, telling Lord Longford that she knew from the bottom of her heart that her sons, Ron and Reg, would never mix with bad people again?'

'I'd forgotten,' said Tudor, 'but it sounds in character all round. I suppose Lord Longford believed her.'

Sanders laughed. 'Self-delusion's fascinating,' he said. 'Gullibility in any shape or form. You'd have to be a shrewd old bird to serve in a British cabinet and yet . . . and what about Violet Kray? Did she believe Ron and Reg would never mix with bad people again?'

Tudor shrugged. 'Mothers don't often believe ill of their offspring. Or rather they don't admit to it.'

'Mmmm. People are always reluctant to believe bad things about people they love. Is that a truism, or a cliché, or even a misconception?'

Tudor looked at the policeman quizzically. 'That's a rather philosophical question for a copper.'

'Do you think so? That's sad. Shall we walk?'

They walked.

A few hundred yards down the road, past a corner shop that reminded Tudor of his childhood – all liquorice allsorts and jars of pear drops and barley sugar – there was a small muncipal park dedicated to the memory of the Duke of Edinburgh – the Victorian version who had planted the first gum tree here with a silver-bladed spade in 1867. The gum tree had flourished along with a myriad of native and imported species, some determinedly homesick for Old England and others aggressively Antipodean, *sui generis* owing nothing to anyone. The garden was neat in the manner of council-controlled open space and yet with a New Frontier element which lifted the dispiriting damper of order, conformity and local politics.

'He's back,' said Tudor, as they passed under the wrought-iron portals and past the statue of the Duke, second son of Queen Victoria and, according to the inscription had not only laid the foundations of this pretty park but had also, in 1862, been elected to the throne of Greece. He 'declined the dignity.'

'Declined the dignity,' murmured Sanders. 'I wish a few more people declined dignity. Life's too full of dignity. It interferes with common sense.Who's back? You mean your friend Professor Carpenter?'

Tudor nodded.

'You surprised?' asked the policeman.

'Not really. But not unsurprised either. Mine is a broadly neutral reaction.'

'Spoken like a professional,' said Sanders. 'Neutrality of reaction is crucial to forensic impartiality. But you're curious?'

'Mildly. Not as curious as I would have been. Or as, perhaps, I should be.'

'Mmmm.' Sanders was chewing something. Gum, presumably, though Tudor would not have been altogether surprised if it turned out to be a wad of tobacco. He had the look of a baseball pitcher with strong biceps – someone perfectly capable of launching a gob of well-aimed brown spittle at an innocent floribunda in the Duke of Edinburgh's Memorial Garden.

'I really wanted to talk some more about what happened last night. To be honest the disappearance and re-emergence of Professor Carpenter is no big deal. Not at the moment anyway. I'm more concerned that we have a sudden unexplained death.'

'I'm all ears.'

'Do you want to sit?' There were park benches all along the paths. Standard issue.

'I'm happy to walk.'

'The forensic tests will take time,' said Sanders, 'but it seems she choked.'

Tudor agreed.

'And my experience is that most people don't just choke. They choke on something. Fishbones, vomit, whatever.'

'I'd prefer to wait for the lab reports but that's my experience certainly.'

'Well,' said Sanders, slowly, seeming to choose his words one by one like a cautious contestant in some TV quiz game, 'the tasting had barely started and Sammy was keeping a pretty close eye on everything. He says that Lorraine only had time to taste one sample.And that sample was yours.'

'I wouldn't know,' said Tudor, 'but I've no reason to dispute it.'

'Hmm.' The two men walked on in silence. The breeze blew chill off the jagged slopes of the Wurlitzer.

'So,' said Sanders, 'she takes one sip of your concoction, goes into spasms and drops down dead in a matter of seconds.'

'If Sammy's right, then yes.' There was no point in arguing with the obvious.

'Cause and effect?'

'Looks awfully like it.'

Sanders hunched his shoulders, the collar of his jacket turned up against the morning cold. A jogger puffed past flat-footed, plugged in to a Walkman. His breathing was heavy and a tinny toccata whispered out of his earphones. It could have been anything from Bach to Beatles, Stockhausen to Spice Girls. The man was a disruption to thought and Sanders and Cornwall covered thirty odd yards before either spoke. This time it was Cornwall.

'If it was my mulled wine that killed Lorraine it must have contained something that was fatal for her but not for anyone else.'

'That's a strange remark,' said Sanders, turning to look at the Visiting Fellow. 'It was only fatal for Lorraine because she was the only person to drink that particular brew. Everyone else sampled something different.'

'Are you sure?'

'That's what Sammy says.'

'And you trust Sammy?' Tudor wasn't trusting anyone at the moment. He saw conspiracy everywhere. He was feeling persecuted and oppressed, perceived no one as being friend, ally or even moderately well-disposed. Not Sammy; not even Greg Sanders, the bright policeman.

'No reason not to,' said Sanders. 'And if it were accidental death then there was something lethal in your concoction which would have affected everyone in the same way. It was just bad luck for Lorraine that she got there first. Could have been any of you.'

'But there wasn't anything universally lethal in my concoction. For God's sake, I mixed it. I know what went into it.'

'Not so fast,' said Sanders. 'You just said that there must have been something in your drink which would only affect Lorraine. Whatever it was wouldn't have killed anyone else.'

'That's not exactly what I said.'

'Let's not quibble.' Was it Tudor's imagination or was the Tasmanian policeman becoming hostile? A new sharpness seemed to have entered his voice. 'If you're right,' Sanders continued, 'then it's a pretty bizarre coincidence, wouldn't you say?'

'If you say so.'

'Well, just for the moment, I do say so.' They had stopped under a weeping gum. The jogger had disappeared over a herbaceous horizon.

Sanders sniffed the scent of the tree, rapt in thought.

'Bizarre coincidences happen. Of course they do. But people in our line of work tend to discount them, don't they?'

'Professional inclination, certainly. But an academic like myself is more inclined to accept the possibility of chance. Life's a pretty random business.'

'Well, I'm a policeman not an academic and just for the moment I'm discounting chance, just as I think you did when you said that whatever it was that killed Lorraine wouldn't have killed anyone else. I think you meant that whatever the substance was, it was introduced deliberately.'

'Not an accident?'

'Not an accident.'

There was a long pause. A magpie warbled. A clock struck the half-hour.

'So,' said Tudor, 'you're suggesting that it was murder.'

Another pause.

'I don't think so,' said Sanders. 'I'm suggesting that when you just said that your mulled wine contained a substance that would kill Lorraine and only Lorraine, then you were suggesting that the substance was introduced deliberately, with the clear intention of inducing a fatal reaction. Making her choke in fact. That's not what I said, it was what *you* were saying.'

Tudor smiled.

'If you were one of my pupils I'd say you were putting words into my mouth. That may have been what you inferred. That's not what I implied.'

'Let's not split hairs.' The inspector's tone was definitely not as friendly as it had been. 'Forget what you said. Pretend it was a slip of the tongue. Now try this for size.'

Suddenly he had slipped back into the voice of one professional discussing a problem with another.

'If someone wanted to kill Lorraine then poison is one of the options.'

'Rare,' interrupted Tudor. 'Poisoning's almost unknown these days.In real life. In real death.'

'All the more reason for a sophisticated murderer adopting that method,' said Sanders, 'and after all, we're talking university here. If this is a crime it's not just any old crime. Not even white collar crime. We're talking high table crime here. Hot stuff. A smart university professor is just the type of person who could come up with a poison that could kill his intended victim but no one else.'

'That's nonsense,' said Tudor. 'A Monsignor Knox rule. No one is allowed to introduce a poison unknown to medical science. It's against reason.'

'Knox was laying down rules for writers of crime fiction,' said Sanders. 'Not quite the same. And I didn't say anything about a poison unknown to medical science. I simply said a substance which would prove lethal to Lorraine and Lorraine alone. Doesn't have to be a poison. Not within the precise meaning of the word.'

'One man's poison is another man's meat.'

Sanders smiled appreciatively. 'You could put it like that. A policeman wouldn't, not being of a literary disposition. But talking of meat I missed breakfast and it's awful cold. Would you mind if we found somewhere to get a bite and a hot drink?'

'The idea of a hot drink seems in slightly doubtful taste,' said Cornwall, 'and I've had breakfast. Still . . .' He shivered, 'It *is* a little cold. And if you're about to accuse me of murder I think I'd rather hear the accusation sitting down.'

CHAPTER NINETEEN

They found a café called a Chip off the Old Block just round the corner from a row of Victorian cottages by the park's main entrance. It was an old-fashioned chippy in new-fangled clothes, a pastiche greasy-spoon with enamelled advertisements for long forgotten sauces and bed-time drinks, a fifties' juke box and a large photograph of Winston Churchill waving a cigar and two fingers.

Sanders ordered chips which came with a fried egg and baked beans on a plate which looked as if it had been deliberately chipped as part of the establishment's themey image. The waitress wore jeans and a check shirt and had a rouged and lipsticked face which made her look like part of the chorus in *Oklahoma*.

'False nostalgia's a strange animal,' said Tudor, burning his lips on a half-pint mug of scalding tea. The tea was rough Indian stuff, the sort of char an uncle of his, a retired Gurkha major, used to call servants' tea. He took it black, no sugar.

'The lab should be able to break down the mulls into their constituents,' said Sanders, 'but tell me about yours and why you chose to do one at all. It seems odd. Something of a presumption after you'd only just arrived. And I wouldn't have put you down as the sort of man who would get a kick out of concocting exotic alcoholic beverages. Your friend Ashley, perhaps. But not you.

I'd mark you down as a person who took his pleasures plain and simple.'

Tudor told him what he had used to elevate the Jolly Jumbuck red wine on to a higher plain.

'Wattle!' said the DCI. 'You don't get wattle in the UK. What made you go for wattle? It's indigenous to Oz. It's like a Pom putting 'roo on a barbie.'

Tudor recognized that the time was fast approaching when he was going to have to own up and tell Sanders about the e-mail instructions from Ashley. If that's what they were. However, he told himself, the time was not yet. Like most people caught up in a lie,particularly those who are not accustomed to telling them, he could feel the deceit becoming more and more incriminating as time passed. The time to tell Sanders about the e-mail was at the first opportunity, at their first meeting. Every second that elapsed after that first missed opportunity was time not just lost but actively arraigned against him. He knew this perfectly well, but he was still disinclined to own up just yet. Besides, he had not violated truth, just been economical with it. His guilt, therefore, was less than total. Also, his professional pride when confronted with a puzzle or conundrum, insisted that he solved it on his own, and he was still a long way from a solution.

On the other hand he had no ready explanation for using wattles.

'And Royal Jelly capsules,' he said, hoping this might distract attention from the wattle.

'At least that sounds British,' said Sanders. 'Sort of honey concentrate?'

'Sort of,' Tudor agreed.

Sanders wiped egg yolk from his lips.

'I don't get it,' he said, finally.'I don't understand why you went in for this crazy competition in the first place; and I don't understand why you should use at least one ingredient which is completely alien to the British Isles. If your drink did kill

Lorraine Montagu, and if it was done deliberately, it had to be done by you and I don't see how you could have a motive. You'd only met the unfortunate woman on one occasion. You couldn't possibly have a reason to kill her. Unless you had not just met Lorraine for the first time but had known her somewhere else and come all the way to Tasmania in order to murder her.'

He leant back in his chair, raised his mug to his lips, drank and then gazed through narrowed eyes at the Visiting Fellow.

'I don't get it,' he said at last. 'I admit I'm struggling but it's early days yet. Our cadaver is hardly cold.'

He smiled.

'Tell me what *you* think, oh learned one. You're the goddamned expert.'

Tudor cleared his throat, on the verge of explaining about the e-mail instructions purporting to come from his absent host but he was saved by the bell.

Literally so, for just as he was about to reveal all, the door opened with the tinny ring of a bell designed to evoke some ill-conceived figment of an ill-remembered past and in walked the Professor of Oenology and the Reader in Green Studies. Jazz Trethewey was looking more hippily elfin than ever and Tasman Penhaligon likewise in his role as the not-so-gentle giant. They also looked conspiratorial to the point at which a casual observer might have perceived them to be an item and a clandestine and illicit one at that. Spotting Tudor and Greg Sanders they both started with what could really only have been some form of guilt. Professor Trethewey smiled in an uncomfortable grimacing apology for a greeting and Dr Penhaligon stared frowningly straight over their head at an advertisement for Milo. Obviously discomfited, they headed for a corner table, sat down, and made a studied ploy of staring intently at the menu.

Sanders raised his eyebrows at Cornwall, inviting some response.

'Your guess is as good as mine,' said Tudor. 'You forget I've only just arrived. I'm a stranger in town. New kid on the block. I've hardly met these people.'

'Don't think I hadn't noticed. It's only your novelty value and your international reputation that are keeping you out of serious trouble so far. And I don't know how much longer that's going to be so.'

'You haven't asked about Ashley Carpenter coming back.'

Tudor knew the change of subject was over-obvious but he was hoping that the unexpected arrival of his new colleagues might have disrupted the policeman's thought process even more thoroughly than the jogger in the park. It was observable that though the Chief Inspector seemed bright enough, his mind had a febrile, butterfly quality quite unlike the dogged relentlessness that Tudor had, over the years, come to associate with most professional police detectives. They were like Isaiah Berlin's tortoise. They knew one big thing and this limited but inexorable knowledge often paid dividends in the end. Sanders on the other hand was a Berlin hare. A bit flashy for a pro. Too much speculation, too much dancing around from one theory to another, too clever by half, not enough bottom.

'Should I?' Greg Sanders answered his question with a question, a response which always infuriated Cornwall when it was tried by his students, even though in truth it was what his interactive style of teaching was inclined to encourage.

'You must agree it's odd,' said Cornwall, aware even as he said it that this was the sort of sentence which would never stand up in court. Not the sort of thing one should say to a bright young policeman, even in Tasmania.

'Life's odd. You know that. Lorraine Montagu's dead. That's odd too. But there's a difference of degree, don't you think?'

The Rogers and Hammerstein waitress came over with a coffee pot, smiled winsomely at Sanders and filled his mug. Tudor asked if he could have more tea and she pouted as if to say she supposed so but he'd got a bloody nerve asking. Tudor felt old and far from home.

'You don't think they're connected?' he asked.

'Should I?'

'Well.' Tudor was on the verge of telling Sanders about the e-mails when he was saved by Jazz Trethewey. She pulled up a chair and sat down unbidden. Her sang-froid seemed to have deserted her and she seemed almost dishevelled, nearly flustered.

'There's something I have to say,' she said, breathlessly. She was alone. Penhaligon was still at their table glowering into space. Tudor found it hard to believe that Penhaligon was a doctor of anything – even green studies.

Sanders regarded her levelly over the chipped rim of his cup.

'Shoot,' he said.

'I owe Dr Cornwall an apology,' she said. 'It was meant to be a joke. That's what he said. Never did seem that funny but I thought it was harmless enough. Until last night.'

'Who said what was a joke?' said Sanders, seeming severe, as if his time were being wasted.

'The disappearance,' said Jazz, as if he were a backward member of her first year winemakers' class, 'Ashley's absent-without-leave performance. It was a practical joke.'

'Jokes are supposed to be funny,' said Sanders. 'They're intended to be humorous, meant to have a point. How come performing an unexplained vanishing trick is such a bloody riot? I don't see it.'

Jazz Trethewey flushed. 'The only reason it was funny was because of Dr Cornwall. Ashley told us he was . . . well, he told us he was a typical pompous Pom . . . needed taking down a peg or two. We didn't know any different so we went along with it. Then it turned out that, well . . .' She seemed almost girlishly embarrassed.

'Please,' said Sanders.

'Listen,' she said, 'Penhaligon over there doesn't think I

should be telling you this.I'm not sure I should be telling you either. But at least make it easy for me. I don't have to be here. I don't have to be doing this. I'm helping you, so help me, for Chris'sake!'

'I think,' said Cornwall, 'that the Chief Inspector is more interested in an unexplained death than an illusory disappearance. Personally I'm riveted by what you have to say about Ashley but it's not a police matter. Greg here is trying to explain death. You're giving us a reading on life. He's not interested in that. Murder is about dead people. You want to tell him about Ashley but Ashley is alive whereas Lorraine is dead. *Ergo*, Greg thinks you're wasting his time. You can't blame him.'

Jazz grimaced.

'I'm not trying to waste anyone's time. I'm a professional academic. That means I have an open mind, a curious mind. Academic study is about the resolution of uncertainty. I'm trying to resolve a small mystery. I agree I'm not solving the main problem but there's linkage here. Lorraine's death affects us all, has been affected by us all in turn. I can't prove that Ashley's little joke has anything to do with it but it's a peculiar coincidence to put it mildly.'

'In that case,' said DCI Sanders with asperity, 'we agree. It's a peculiar coincidence. And I'm happy to put it mildly too. But in real life I have more serious things to deal with.'

'That sounds pretty bloody pompous,' said the Professor of Wine. 'You have an unexpected, unexplained sudden death; you have an unexpected, unexplained sudden disappearance and you rule out the possibility of any connection between the two without even listening to what I have to tell you.'

The policeman finished his coffee.

'Look,' he said, 'I have things to discuss with Dr Cornwall. You obviously have things to discuss with Dr Cornwall. May I suggest that you allow me to finish my discussion with him and then you can take over and have your own discussion?'

Professor Trethewey glared, thought for a moment, then rose and stomped off wordlessly to Tasman Penhaligon who glowered still but looked like a man vindicated.

'Did you have to be quite so rude?' asked Tudor, when she was out of earshot.

'Best policy,' said Sanders laconically. 'I know her sort: give her half a chance and she'd take over the whole investigation. Most of the world thinks it would make a better job of being a policeman than the police. You know that. In a way' – and he smiled – 'you and your sort are the worst offenders. But at least you're a specialist even if your expertise is academic. People like Professor Trethewey are intellectually superior ignoramuses.Pain in the bum. I wouldn't challenge her on her own subject so I don't see why she should challenge me on mine.'

'I doubt that,' said Cornwall. 'I bet you're even more of a wine "expert" than she is a crime "expert." "Anything but Chardonnay." "Amused by its presumption." Be fair. She was only trying to help. I happen to think she may also be right. I think there may well be a connection between Ashley going AWOL and Lorraine choking on the mulled wine.'

Sanders sighed and made check-signing motions at the waitress.

'With respect,' he said, 'even you are not exempt from the idea that detection is based on the sort of intuitive processes which fuel fiction. I'm not Sherlock Holmes much less Hercule Poirot. Little grey cells are crucial but they work with modern science. The lab reports will solve this little mystery.'

He grinned as the jeansy waitress brought the bill.

'The lab reports are going to tell me exactly what you put in the drink. Once I know that I'll know how Lorraine Montagu died. And why.'

'That I doubt,' said Tudor, also irritated.

They pushed back their chairs and went. Sanders did not acknowledge the two academices whose malevolent gaze followed their departure. Cornwall however allowed himself a more or less furtive glance and a fleeting smile at Professor Trethewey. His gesture was acknowledged, just as fleetingly, just as furtively.

CHAPTER TWENTY

Cornwall and the detective parted company at the entrance to the college. They did so on terms which could be best described as scratchy. Over the years Tudor had often found his relations with the police uneasy. They respected his knowledge and his opinions but there was, nearly always, a strong element of the 'those that can, do, those that can't, teach.'

Even at home the chief constable, whom he had known for years and regarded as a friend, would, on occasion, say 'Tudor, it's one thing to solve crimes in your ivory tower, dreaming away with your learned papers and academic theories, but it's quite another to do it in real life. When you're working at the-coal face, murder takes on a rather different complexion.'

Or words to that effect.

And after years of trying, Tudor had more or less given up the struggle. He believed passionately in the value of the university, in learning for learning's sake, in the contribution to be made by thought and research and study away from the constraints and limitations of what the chief constable called 'Real Life'. 'Real Life' in his book was a messy business which, left to its own devices, would always end in tears. It needed the cool light of reason and knowledge to improve it and miners at the rock face like the chief constable – a particularly inapposite simile in the chief constable's case – needed the corrective insights of intellects like his.

Men and women like the chief constable however, never listened let alone understood these arguments and so nowadays Tudor would simply shrug and hope that in due course he would be able to demonstrate that he had a point.

So, outside St Petroc's, he smiled a wispy, half-defeated little smile and said that he wished DCI Sanders well in his endeavours and looked forward to hearing from him again when he had the report from the lab. He sensed, more than usual, that the policeman was torn between admiration for his work and resentment of his intrusion. At least Sanders read the learned journals, was aware of his well-researched and rigorously argued papers and articles. That made a pleasant change. Tudor also sensed that Sanders suspected him of being economic with the facts, of telling him less than the whole truth. In this, of course, he was correct, and Tudor felt a pang of guilt as well as being uncertain about why he was concealing the matter of the e-mails. He would have to own up in the end but before he did he wanted to be more sure about what precisely it was that he was owning up to.

Oh, for a simple life! This was supposed to be a sabbatical. Featherweight teaching duties. Accessibility to students in an undemanding, sociable, drink-at-the-bar sort of way. All port and pleasantry.

'So when forensics have done their stuff I'll be in touch,' said Sanders. 'I'll value your thoughts, I really will.'

'Of course,' said Tudor. 'Anything I can do to help.'

'I appreciate it,' said Sanders, then hesitated. 'I don't mean any offence,' he said, 'but I think you're caught up in this – whatever it is. You can't do the omniscient detached professor act this time. You're involved, however obliquely. And, like I say, I mean no offence but you may need help as much as I do. Only in a different way.'

Tudor shivered involuntarily. They were his thoughts precisely. Rather more precisely indeed than his own thoughts which were still uncharacteristically inarticulate. Trust a bright copper to cut through the crap.

'Thanks,' he said, 'I appreciate what you're saying. You're right. It's a novel experience and not one I'm entirely happy with.'

'I can see that,' said Sanders. 'So don't forget: a problem shared is a problem halved. Or whatever.'

They shook hands. The gesture was oddly formal. Tudor was not much given to shaking hands. Physical contact of all kinds was something about which he was unusually fastidious. As the policeman finally walked away Tudor found himself looking down at his fingers with distaste, almost as if they might have been contaminated.

Then he heard his name being called and realized he was daydreaming.

'Sorry, Sammy,' he said, almost physically pulling himself together, 'I was somewhere else.'

'Wish I was, sir,' said Sammy, grinning. 'Message from the Principal. She wants to see you. In the Lodge. Whenever you can make it. She said it was urgent. Doesn't mind being disturbed.'

'Right you are, Sammy,' he said. 'Any idea what it's about?'

'Your guess is as good as mine.'

Like many people in his position, thought Tudor, Sammy teetered on the brink of insolence. This was, he acknowledged, a ridiculous thought in this egalitarian age and he would have been revolted if anyone thought he craved deference. Yet there was a difference between deference and respect. Respect was what premiership football clubs gave each other. It wouldn't have come amiss from the college servant.

Jesus, he said to himself. Tudor, stop being so pompous. No

wonder they're playing practical jokes on you.

He wondered if Dame Edith was in on the act. On balance he thought not.

CHAPTER TWENTY-ONE

She was painting when he entered after a tentative knock had been greeted with a stentorian 'Come!' She was sitting at an easel wearing a tattered, oil-stained, tangerine-coloured smock and a green beret which looked more Royal Marine Commando than Montmartre. The same might be said of its owner even if she were demonstrably past her prime.

Tudor approached the easel and was impressed. The Dame was painting an echidna and doing so with an immaculate technique and precision that was in apparent conflict with what Tudor had too readily dismissed as the scattiness of the archetypal don. He had forgotten that she had once excelled in the cut-throat trade of politics. Also that she was internationally respected in her area of science. The picture wasn't what a critic would have called art but it was a meticulous representation of what these small antipodean hedgehoggy-porcupines actually looked like.At least that was how it seemed to Cornwall. He had yet to actually see an echidna in the wild but he was convinced by Dame Edith's rendition.

'Brilliant!' said Cornwall, trying not to sound patronizing but only half-succeeding.

'I'm no Lucien Freud,' she said, 'nor even Grandma Moses or

Mabel Lucy Attwell, but for what they are they could hardly be bettered.'

'I don't doubt it.' Cornwall was not sure of his place but wherever it was he definitely felt put in it.

'Do you know anything about art?'

'Well . . .' He took what he considered an intelligent layman's interest but was swept aside before he could explain it.

'Or echidnas?'

'We don't have echidnas in the United Kingdom. Hedgehogs.'

'I don't suppose you know the first thing about hedgehogs either,' she said testily, 'but why should you? It's a relatively arcane subject which I happen to have made my own. Everyone to their last. I know nothing about Jack the Ripper or Osama Bin Laden which you obviously do. It's a matter of taste.'

Tudor wasn't sure about this but this was not the moment to pick a fight.

'In any event, you can take it from me that as a representation of an echidna this is as good as it gets. Besides, I find that painting eases stress, and at the moment I'm feeling exceedingly stressed. My stress levels have risen dramatically since you arrived on the scene and I'm bound to say that the two strike me as likely to be closely related.'

Tudor began to expostulate but she cut him short.

'I know, I know. It's not your fault.'

She didn't sound particularly convinced.

'Look.' She got up from her stool, set down her brush and re-established herself at the leathery chair behind her partner's desk. There she paused and gazed at him appraisingly, as if seeing him for the first time.

'I'm not getting any younger.'

Tudor was tempted to say either 'You could have fooled me', or 'Which of us is?', but felt that either response was inadvisable. All the same he never ceased to be amazed by the shallows of banality in which great minds so frequently became beached.

He said nothing.

'I have been minded to retire for some little while.'

Who did she think she was? Queen Elizabeth the First?

'One of the several problems with running an organization of any kind is that there are so few people in whom one can confide. It has been as difficult to be entirely honest with the Fellows of St Petroc's as it used to be with my fellow Cabinet ministers in my days of government.'

She paused, partly for effect, and partly to expectorate in an emphysymatic manner which called for a spittoon though one was not available. A cat on the sofa jerked awake and looked at her reproachfully.

'I used to talk to Lorraine,' she said.

For a moment she seemed uncharacteristically affected. A red and white spotted handkerchief was withdrawn from one of the smock's capacious sleeves and dabbed to damely cheeks.

'As non-academic staff,' she said, 'Lorraine was the only person of any intelligence and experience at St Petroc's with whom I could discuss my retirement. Everyone else viewed themselves, reasonably or not, as a potential successor. Because of this I naturally had to play my cards close to my chest.'

Cornwall had a sudden nightmarish vision of being clasped to that capacious camphor-scented bosom and winced despite himself.

She gave him a sharp but uncomprehending look.

'Now that Lorraine has been taken from us in such a dramatic and unexpected manner, I have no one in whom I can safely confide. Except perhaps you.'

Cornwall nodded. He too could play cards close to his chest. He said nothing.

'May I trust you?'

'Absolutely.'

'Well you would say that, wouldn't you?'

This was true and once more silence seemed the only response.

'I suppose we must suspect what in your neck of the academic woods you doubtless refer to as foul play?'

'It's not for me to say,' said Cornwall cautiously. 'The police seem perfectly competent. More than usually so I'd judge. DCI Sanders seems particularly bright.'

'Don't care for the cut of his jib,' said the Dame.

Cornwall guessed she was referring to his dress code, or lack of one. Sanders was not someone who would pass sartorial muster at high table.

'That's by the way,' she said. 'Between you and me I was on the verge of announcing my retirement but with the college in such turmoil it seems hardly the time. What do you think?'

'Probably not,' said Cornwall. 'St Petroc's has enough going on without a leadership election to contend with.'

'Quite so. I'm sure Lorraine would have thought the same, God bless her. Naturally the issue is complicated by the fact that at least two of the Fellows regard themselves as contenders for the job.'

'Ashley and Jazz Trethewey?'

The Dame shot him a sharp look which suggested he had risen a notch in her estimation though from a low base.

'Brad is far too young and Tasman Penhaligon far too mad,' she said.

'But you came from outside? It doesn't have to be an internal candidate?'

'Correct.' She smiled the sort of smile the TV compere would reserve for the weakest link. 'But I was a St Petroc's girl: I had a certain standing in both the public and academic worlds, and though I shouldn't admit it, there were no other serious candiates. The college tradition is that the Principal comes alternately from within and without. Having myself been a Petrockian but not a collegiate candidate I count as an outsider. Unless we depart from tradition the next Principal must be drawn from the Fellowship.'

'Which, in effect, means Jazz or Ashley.'

'Precisely so.'

'And now, suddenly you don't fancy either of them as your successor.'

'Well, young man, the words nail and head spring speedily to mind. So what do you propose?'

Saying which she leant back and waited.

'It may not seem so to you,' said Dame Edith, 'but in this part of the world St Petroc's is regarded as rather a plum. It may seem fanciful but I think I'm not exaggerating if I suggest that both Jazz and Ashley would die for it.'

'Which is not the same as saying that they would kill for it,' said Cornwall.

'I don't think this is a moment for flippancy,' she said.

Tudor hadn't meant to seem flippant. He bit his tongue and buttoned his lip.

'Until the other day Ashley would have been my preferred candidate. Now I'm not so sure. As for Professor Trethewey she has much to commend her, but . . . But.'

It was such a little word but ejected from the Principal's puckered lips, such a damning one as well.

'I'll be frank,' she said.

Cornwall nodded.

'Until a week or so ago I would have said I knew Ashley Carpenter quite well.' She looked plaintive. 'I'm not sure whether I believe in the male menopause but if there is such a thing I'd say Ashley was going through it. I don't think he was treating poor Lorraine at all well though she never complained.'

'Did she say anything?'

'Not a word. Whenever I tried to get her to open up she changed the subject. She was very open and honest with me about most things but definitely not about Ashley. And then there's Ashley's relationship with this little minx Elizabeth Burney. I simply don't know what's been going on there. Ashley maintains he's simply been taking a paternal interest in her, acting as her moral tutor. Says he feels sorry for her. Just because she's barely out of her teens doesn't mean to say she can't run rings round someone as goofy as Ashley. Oh dear.'

Tudor suddenly felt sorry for the old bat. She didn't deserve all this hassle at her time of life. One of the cats yawned and stretched.

'And then he goes wandering off up the Wurlitzer without telling anyone and then reappears without so much as a by-your-leave. What do you make of it?'

'I don't know,' said Tudor truthfully. 'It's been suggested that it might have been some form of practical joke.'

'I've always loathed practical jokes,' said the Dame, standing up again, walking purposefully to her painting and staring at it intently with beetling brows. 'Extraordinarily pleasant temperaments, echidnas,' she said. 'Hedgehogs too. Far more agreeable than humans. If I had my life again I'd have been one. And I'd certainly have devoted more time to them. Human beings, have, on the whole, been a terrible disappointment. Don't you agree?'

'I suppose so.'

She sat down again, heavily. 'So what do you think? Was poor Lorraine murdered? If so how and by whom? Did Ashley vanish of his own accord or was he abducted? If so, why in both cases and by whom in the latter?'

'Who had a plausible motive for murdering Lorraine?'

The Dame chewed her lip.

'Lorraine had been here a long time. She and I discussed confidential matters. Everyone knew that. She knew where the skeletons were buried, to borrow that unfortunate phrase.'

'Were there a lot of skeletons?'

'There are always skeletons in a community like this. She knew more than I did. She told me a little about them, it's true, but only what she felt I needed to know. She also had the ear of the governing body. More than me I'm afraid, and that's important.'

'Why so?'

'Like most governing bodies they're a rubber stamp outfit but they do technically vote in the new Principal. It's customary to listen to my recommendations, but they don't have to pay the slightest attention.But they liked Lorraine. We all liked Lorraine.'

The Principal sniffed.

'I warned her about becoming entangled with Ashley but she wouldn't listen. She said she was afraid of life passing her by. I think she had me in her sights as a matter of fact but that's another story. She didn't fancy being an old maid like me. My advice was that she was better off with echidnas than Ashley but—'

'Are you suggesting that Ashley was . . . unreliable or . . . what exactly are you suggesting?'

'May I be frank?'

'You are.' At least he thought she was. It could have been some sort of bluff.

'I know that Ashley is a very old friend of yours.'

'I'm beginning to have my doubts.' This was true and frank. He felt he owed it to her.

'What I said about the male menopause,' she said, 'I think that may be true whatever it means. But I have a feeling that it may be more significant than that. My sense is that Ashley is suddenly coming to terms with failure. Succeeding me in this post, unglamorous as I'm sure it seems to you, is a last throw of the dice for him. Quite suddenly he's realized that if he doesn't get this there's nothing left. He's never going to write that great book; he's never going to be awarded that prestigious chair in Criminal Studies at Harvard or Yale or Oxford or Cambridge.Principal of St Petroc's would give him a platform, a handle. It may not be All Souls or even Massey College but it has a certain cachet. Ashley could use it as a passport to greater things and it would reassure him that his achievements are not as second-rate as he fears.'

Cornwall frowned.

'So Ashley was unduly keen to succeed you. That's not a crime. Ambition is usually regarded as healthy.'

'Not if it becomes obsessive.'

Tudor had little craving for title or rank. He loved his work with a passion and wanted only to do it to the limit of his abilities. That was reward in itself. He understood that others needed recognition whether from their peers or the world at large but his understanding was theoretical rather than emotional. He saw that others acted from different motivations, their clocks ticking from a different spring as it were. But he didn't quite get it. It was what made him such a good academic. He was easily able to take the dispassionate over-view, never became over-sympathetic to his subject.

'So?' he asked.

'So nothing,' said the Dame. 'I'm thinking out loud and I'm using you as a sounding board. A response or two would be welcome but is not essential. That's not the point of the exercise. I need to order my thoughts and I find it helpful to have a second party to assist in that enterprise. It was what Lorraine was so adept at.'

'What you seem to be saying,' said Cornwall, 'is that Ashley is going off the rails. But it's all hunch and hypothesis.'

'Not entirely,' she said. 'First of all he develops a relationship with Lorraine. Not done. You don't sleep with other members of the same organization if you're unmarried. Particularly if it's an academic institution.'

'Isn't that a rather old-fashioned view?'

'I *am* old-fashioned. So is St Petroc's. So is Tasmania.'

'Even so,' said Cornwall, 'the world is changing. Senior common room sex is a fact of life. It always was, if the truth be told. It's just that the past was a different country. Discreet. Unknowable. Everything that went on in bed was swept under it. If you follow.'

'That's still true here. But in addition to Lorraine there was this extraordinary business with the Burney girl which I simply can't fathom. I don't know if sex has been involved but even someone as apparently broad-minded as you must accept that for a tutor to sleep with one of his students is not just a betrayal of trust, it's simply asking for trouble. He should never even have looked at her. You know that.'

Cornwall did. He had been tempted but never succumbed. Several of his female students had been eighteen going on thirty-five, bent on mischief and seduction. In the old days one might have got away with it. Besides, many of the cases he'd known about were thoroughly satisfactory all round – reassuring for middle-aged dons and revelatory for teenage girls. Some had even gone on to contract happy marriages. But in these days of feminism and political correctness it was a bad move. A lot of these vampish students were heavily into entrapment.

'And then this ridculous going off into the far blue yonder.'

'Quite.' Cornwall certainly wasn't going to disagree about Ashley's tiresome vanishing trick.

'So all-in-all Ashley's queered his pitch as far as taking over the college is concerned.'

'Thus opening up the way for Jazz Trethewey?'

Dame Edith rubbed at one of many paint-spots on her grubby smock.

'You might think so but I'm afraid I have reservations about Professor Trethewey. Difficult to put one's finger on it. Several of the governing body think the same. There's also some pressure to make a male appointment.'

'But hang on.' Cornwall was puzzled. 'If Ashley is really so keen to succeed you then why does he do three things which seem perfectly calculated to prevent him? After all, if he did succeed to the Principal's position he could indulge his *droit de seigneur* as much as he wanted and go for unannounced walkabouts whenever he wished.'

'I wouldn't bank on that,' said Dame Edith. 'There is a long history of sexual abuse by the heads of residential colleges and others in exalted positions. Generally speaking the higher you go the harder you fall.'

Tudor rubbed his jaw. 'There's another way of looking at it. Having an affair with Lorraine would mean that she was on-side with the powers-that-be which would help his candidature. Getting involved with Elizabeth Burney could be construed as taking a genuine interest in student welfare. Going off for an unscheduled short leave could be interpreted as an interesting spiritual exercise. Like going into retreat. Contemplation, solitude, space . . . all rather attractive in a serious academic. Welcome change from committee-fixated academic bureaucrats.'

'Without letting anyone know?'

'Spontaneity's an academic rarity too, but I'm sure Ashley could propound it as a virtue.'

The Dame arched an eyebrow and kicked out vaguely at a cat which was rubbing against her sensible shoe.

'All right, I'm playing Devil's advocate,' he said, 'but he could have been thinking like that. Especially if you're right and he is a touch menopausal.'

The Dame seemed doubtful.

'If you put it like that,' she said, 'it does seem faintly plausible, but not for long.'

'Have you talked to him about all this?'

She looked discomfited, as well, Tudor felt, she might.

'Not properly. I suppose I'm losing my touch. One reason I want to resign and spend more time on my echidnas. It simply doesn't seem worth the candle. Confrontation, unpleasantness, raised voices. I've reached an age when I feel entitled to a quiet life. I suppose I thought being head of a residential college of the University of Tasmania would provide just the tranquillity I crave. Peaceful old age.'

She shook her head ruefully.

'It's not too late.'

'I suppose not. But you, too, you have things you need to discuss with your old friend.'

'Yes,' he said. He had much more to discuss with Ashley than the old girl realized, 'Later this morning. Shouldn't you talk to Jazz?'

'I don't think we have anything to talk about. Not if I defer my retirement. Which I have to do.'

'And the police. They have to be talked to.'

For a moment Cornwall was afraid Dame Edith was going to crumple. There was a momentary unstiffening of the lip, a moistness of the eye, but in seconds she pulled herself together.

'The police,' she said. 'I detest having the police on campus. It's an invasion, an intrusion. Our privacy is being violated.'

Cornwall felt obliged to venture a protest.

'Dame Edith,' he said, 'there was a violent and unexplained death in the college less than twenty-four hours ago. That's a police matter. You know that. You'd be much more concerned if the police weren't here doing a difficult job to the best of their ability. I'm sure they appreciate your concerns.I think they're well aware of the special nature of the college and all it stands for. Nevertheless in a well-ordered society we need a responsible police force. They're here to enforce the law which is the difference between a civilized society and chaos.'

For a moment he was afraid he had jeopardized the cordiality built up over the last few moments, but to his relief, she laughed and said simply, 'For a second I'd forgotten your calling in life, Dr Cornwall. You can keep that sort of lecture for your first-year criminal studies students.' Then, growing serious, she looked at him pleadingly, and said, 'You do think it was an accident, don't you?'

Cornwall looked her in the eyes and knew she didn't think it had been an accident either.

'Murder,' he said. 'That's what I think. Proving it will be

something else again. But now, if you'll excuse me, I have a class to teach.'

Oddly, she seemed reassured by this, and he left feeling he had done a good deed, though little clearer in his mind about what exactly his old friend Ashley Carpenter was playing at.

CHAPTER TWENTY-TWO

He read his class the first short story of G.K. Chesterton's *The Innocence of Father Brown*. There were a dozen students and they seemed pleasantly baffled. From time to time he stopped to ask them what the author meant by phrases such as 'He was smoking a cigarette with the seriousness of an idler' or a 'celibate simpleton.' The answers were fumbled but polite. He got the impression that they were enjoying the sound he was making and were indifferent to the meaning of the words he was using. The class had never heard of a Eucharistic Congress and were unfamiliar with Liverpool Street or Hampstead Heath. Cornwall, in this faraway place of which he knew less and less, was soothed by such references and by the gentle surreality of Chesterton's conceits.

'So,' he said, when he had finished, 'the myopic little priest from Essex has proved superior to Valentin, head of the Paris police, the most famous investigator in the world. What do you make of that?'

There was a silence. Elizabeth Burney was not in this class. Cornwall was not sure whether she should have been. In fact, he had a very imprecise idea of who should be there. Attendance at class seemed to be a more elastic concept than what he was used to.

'What's myopic mean?'

'Sorry,' he said. 'Short-sighted. Father Brown was short-sighted. At least he affected short-sight. Remember, Chesterton tells us that he can't tell one end of a railway ticket from another. Personally I suspect that he wasn't as short-sighted as he makes out. It's a classic disguise, isn't it? It makes us believe that he was a simpleton. Any physical disability has the same effect on the onlooker, wouldn't you say? Despite all the obvious evidence to the contrary, we equate physical inadequacies with mental ones.'

There was a certain amount of shuffling and staring at the floor. Every one of the students had a writing implement poised above a pad or notebook of some kind but very few had actually written anything.

'You know,' he tried again, 'that if you're confronted with someone in a wheelchair you're inclined to talk very loudly or very slowly because you think their comprehension has been impaired just like his mobility.'

'Stephen Hawking's in a wheelchair and he's just about the cleverest man in the world,' said a boy in a vivid check shirt with a close-cropped head and rings through his nose.

'Yeah,' said a girl with thick glasses, 'but Hawking admits that if you have slurred speech people think you're mentally deficient. Which is why his speech synthesizer is so brilliant.'

'Who's Stephen Hawking?' asked a blonde at the back.

'He wrote *A Brief History of Time*, dumbo,' said the youth with the ringed nose.

'What does any of this have to do with the stuff Tudor's been reading us?'

Cornwall seized his chance. Not patronizing students was a cardinal rule. They had a limitless capacity for surprise as well as disappointment. He thought of saying that this class looked so stupid that they couldn't possibly have heard of Stephen Hawking but thought better of it.

'Chesterton,' he said, 'created a detective with very short-sight, a vacuous expression and a clumsy manner. He also made him a Roman Catholic Priest. Then he christened him Brown, which is as ordinary and unremarkable a name as you can imagine. It's such a good disguise that even Valentin, the world's greatest policeman, and Flambeau, the world's greatest criminal, are fooled. They don't realize that Father Brown is actually a great detective.'

One or two of the class scribbled a sentence or so. Tudor wondered what.

'At the time,' said Cornwall, 'purists complained that Father Brown flouted all the conventions and relied on something totally different – a combination of intuition and priestliness. How does he know in that story I just read you, that the priest isn't really a priest?'

The boy with the rings stuck up a hand and when Tudor nodded he said 'Because he attacked reason and he said that was bad theology.'

'Absolutely,' said Cornwall, pleased. 'Only someone who knew their theology would have spotted that. And how many real-life police detectives know anything about theology? Or modern fictional ones come to that?'

A slim, sexy figure slipped into a seat at the back of the room and put up a hand. Elizabeth Burney.

'Sorry I'm late,' she said. 'I was working the breakfast shift. Are you saying you solve mysteries by guesswork?'

'I'm saying,' Tudor spoke deliberately, choosing his words carefully, 'that a hundred or so years ago, G.K. Chesterton could invent a more or less plausible detective who solved many of his crimes by what modern professional detectives would describe as guesswork. But we have to remember that Chesterton's generation didn't have the scientific apparatus available to us in the twenty-first century.'

'So,' smiled little Miss Burney, 'there's no room for hunches and guesswork any longer?'

'I didn't quite say that,' he said. 'You're putting words into my mouth. What I am saying is that the successful detective in this or any other age is like the creative artist. He has to be capable of leaps of the imagination which even he or she may not fully understand.'

'So who killed Mrs Montagu is down to guesswork?'

She smiled, a picture of innocence.

Cornwall was determined not to be fazed.

'We shouldn't be talking about the tragic death of Miss Montagu so soon after the event. However, since you raised the matter, I'll make one point and one point only: the modern, real-life, professional detective will determine the cause and circumstances of death according to scientific evidence. Chesterton's Father Brown would have come to his conclusion in a quite different, almost spiritual manner.' He looked at the girl meaningfully. 'But I'm quite sure they would both have got there in the end.'

She simpered but said nothing.

'I'd like you all to have read at least half-a-dozen Father Brown short stories by the time we next meet,' he said, 'and I'll expect you to be able to produce a convincing critique of his methodology. If that's what it is.'

He snapped his book shut.

'And now, I'm sorry, but I have an appointment,' he said.

Actually he had ten minutes or so before he was due to meet Ashley but he needed to collect his thoughts by pacing about in the quad. Reading Chesterton and Father Brown reminded him, inevitably, of the words of Monsignor Ronald Knox.

There once was a man who said God
Must think it exceedingly odd
If he finds that this tree
Continues to be
When there's no one about in the Quad.

Knox, he recalled, had propounded the *Decalogue*, that famous and witty set of ten commandments for those who wrote detective fiction. Unlike Father Brown he was a real-life Roman Catholic priest. Also, unlike Father Brown, he wore his cleverness on his sleeve, flaunting it for all to see. Ashley, he remembered, always disliked Roman Catholics having been brought up a Methodist. He also affected a disdain for fictional crime, much preferring the real thing, whereas Cornwall tried to keep the two in balance. It was this compound of fact and fiction which made his criminal studies course so unusual if not unique.

How odd of God, he thought to himself, gazing up at a huge eucalyptus in the centre of the quadrangle. Gum trees were so profoundly un-English. Why had God put them on this side of the globe and not the other? Why had God put him into this situation? *Had* God put him into this situation? If he were Father Brown or Ronnie Knox he would have sought Divine inspiration but, in truth, his religious tendencies were agnostic. 'Sorry God!' he said, 'I'm not sure I believe in you. Particularly now. You've sent me halfway round the world in order to fall out with my oldest friend . . . no, that was an exaggeration. Maybe it is too early to tell but it is not looking good.'

He tried rehearsing the impending interview.

'Now look here, Ashley, there's no one else to hear, so you can be absolutely frank. If there's something on your mind you can tell me. After all, we've known each other long enough. No secrets between friends as old as us, surely?'

That wouldn't quite do.

He tried again.

'Ashley, I haven't told a soul about those peculiar e-mails you sent when you were missing. Don't ask me why not but I felt I owed you something. I'm not so sure now. Explain, please. Surely you owe me that.'

That wasn't right either.

'Ashley, you were having an affair with Lorraine Montagu.

You instruct me to mix a mulled wine brew. She takes a gulp and drops down dead. The following morning you reappear as suddenly as you vanished. I think you've got some explaining to do.'

That was nearer the nub of the matter.

He could add in some stuff about Elizabeth Burney.

'And the college has one girl who seems to be the ultimate kleptomaniac, nymphomaniac and heaven knows what else. Who seems to have got himself entangled with her but you? What do you mean by it?'

While he was at it he could take the offensive over the vanishing trick as well.

'You invite me all this way and do a bunk leaving me to be met by this kid called Brad Davey who hasn't a clue what's going on any more than I have. So what in God's name is this all about?'

Tudor smiled to himself. There was God, creeping unbidden into his thoughts again. There was no keeping the Almighty at bay sometimes. But whatever else He might be He was not one of the Great Detectives. Part of Great Detection was trying to discern God's purpose. Indeed, you could argue, could you not, that in that sense God was on the opposite side to the detective. He had all the answers, yet concealed them from sleuths amateur and professional.Tudor would have liked the sort of hotline to God enjoyed by Fathers Knox and Brown, but this was not vouchsafed him, precluded by his innate scepticism.

'Oh God!' he said, out loud, and laughed. But it wasn't a laughing matter. His best friendship was in jeopardy. A woman had died suddenly. He was implicated, was withholding information, possibly vital. In a few minutes he had to get the truth out of Ashley and he didn't know how.

'Ashley, old friend, you're not yourself. Tell me what's wrong. I want to help. I'm your friend. Tell me, Ashley.'

Could Jazz Trethewey's truncated allegation in the greasy spoon be true? That Ashley had lured him here in order to make fun of him, to ridicule him for his Pommish pomposity. That wasn't much of a joke. Maybe Tudor had lost his sense of humour. He had to concede that it had never been at its strongest when he himself was the butt of the joke. But who in the world really was good at laughing at themselves? And what was the nature of the joke? OK, Tudor, here's a real-life mystery, get off your academic high horse and solve something real for once. Maybe. But Ashley was a crime academic too. People in glass houses shouldn't throw bricks. If he was making a point about ivory tower dwelling, dreaming-spired university professors being out of touch with the real world, then he was the wrong person to make it. He was as much of a dreamer as the rest of his profession.

He tried once more.

'The truth, Ashley. Just tell me the truth.'

All those years ago when they had been undergraduates together they had been honest with each other, never told lies, never kept secrets. They had known each other inside out and that had formed the basis for a life-long friendship.

Hadn't it? Well, hadn't it?

CHAPTER TWENTY-THREE

His plans proved futile as, on reflection, they usually did where Ashley was concerned. However well laid they might be – and these weren't – Ashley always seemed to take the initiative. It had been ever thus. Tudor had never noticed this before but now for the first time in their long relationship he was suspicious and questioning. Suddenly everything that he had taken for granted seemed disturbing and odd. Rightly or wrongly the trust was gone. Even a smile or a handshake was a cause for concern. He didn't like it.

'Tudor, old bean!' said Ashley, standing in his open doorway with Basil wagging his tail at his feet. He had always called Tudor 'old bean' at university though neither man could remember exactly how or why. Something to do with having read Frank Richards' Greyfriars stories as boys.

'Ashley, old fruit!' said Tudor, through force of habit rather than conviction. This too had been his greeting to his friend when they were students and they had gone on like it ever since, though not, for preference, in front of other people.

'Come in, come in.' Ashley was warm as an open fire though Tudor in his new mood of wariness, wondered if he wasn't one of the modern generation of gas jobs, the ones with the movable lumps of uninflammable coals that looked just like the real

McCoy until you threw a cigarette end or sweet paper on to it. Warm but artifically so. More light than heat.

'I've got a bottle on ice,' said Ashley. 'A sparkling red infuriator. All the rage in these parts.'

Tudor recognized the prancing stallion logo of the Rymill winery. Their fizzy Shiraz was becoming as ubiquitous as the spooky Elizabeth Burney.

'Ah,' he said.

Basil jumped up at him, tail wagging ferociously.

Tudor bent down and scratched behind the dog's ears.

'G'day Bazza!' he said. 'Who's a good boy?'

'Basil seems to have taken a shine to you,' said Ashley. He didn't sound very amused about it.

'He's been a good friend right from the moment we met. Gave me a really warm welcome. Which is more than can be said for one or two others.'

Tudor could hardly have been more pointed but Ashley did not acknowledge the rebuke. Instead he said, 'Take a pew. Have a drink. Relax. Put your feet up.' He cleared a pile of papers from the sofa and gestured at the vacated space. 'Make yourself at home.'

'Thanks.'

Having surrendered the initiative, Tudor reckoned the best stance was the staccato or even the silent. If he said nothing or as little as possible there was a greater chance of Ashley saying something which with luck would turn into more than he intended. Particularly if he were feeling guilty.

Ashley proffered a glass of sparkling red. They both said 'Cheers' and sipped. Tudor stayed stumm and after a pause Ashley said, 'I suppose I owe you an apology.'

'I suppose so,' said Tudor, wishing he hadn't. It sounded sarcastic. Silence would have been better. He kicked himself metaphorically.

'Well, I'm sorry. Though it seems you've been well looked after.'

Tudor obeyed his own instructions to himself, had another sip and frowned into his glass.

'The fact is that I needed some time and space.'

A long and awkward silence which gave them both time and space.

Basil whimpered.

Ashley filled the gap.

'I've been having a difficult time.'

Tudor had no immediate wish to make it easier.

'Women for one thing.' Ashley looked sheepish. 'Never a very strong point with me, as you know.'

Tudor said nothing. There seemed nothing to say. The matter of Ashley and women was not something that had ever caused him loss of sleep or even an idle moment. Not that he was a prey to many idle moments.

'You had it off with Miranda didn't you?'

This *did* demand some sort of response, a question coming from a long way left of centre and a generation too late.

'You what?' he said, idiotically.

Ashley stared at his glass and reddened as if in sympathy.

'Doesn't matter,' he said.

'Well it obviously does.' Tudor frowned. This was ancient history, another world, another life. Sex had barely been invented and neither had experienced any with Miranda. That was the point. It was this shared failure which had spawned their relationship. But it no longer had anything to do with anything. At least not as far as Tudor was concerned.

'I said it doesn't matter.' Ashley's voice sounded unnaturally strained.

He sipped wine and made a visible effort to pull himself together.

'Anyway, old chap. I'm awfully sorry. Failing in my duty as a host. All got a bit much for me.'

Tudor judged sympathy was called for though he wasn't feeling much.

'Care to talk about it?' he offered, gingerly.

'Not really, old man. Private, personal. Bit embarrassing to tell the truth. But it's water under the bridge now.'

'You and Lorraine?'

Ashley shot him a sharp, hostile glance.

'What do you know about me and Lorraine?'

'Only what everyone else seems to know. And what she told me herself.'

'Nobody else knows anything. It's a private matter. *Was* a private matter.'

Ashley's voice had risen several octaves again. He poured himself more wine and more too for Tudor, though the level in Tudor's glass had barely fallen.

Taken to drink, Tudor said to himself, recognizing as he did that the thought was prissy and based on nothing. Ashley had always liked a jar. Himself as well. But it was no more than social drinking. Well, wasn't it? Always perfectly under control. Ashley's hands were shaking. He was obviously stressed.

'Cigarette?' Ashley asked.

'I didn't think you smoked,' said Tudor, trying to keep a critical note out of his voice. He wasn't critical. If people wanted to kill themselves by kippering that was their affair. He knew he sounded censorious even though he didn't mean to. But that wasn't the point. The point was that he knew bloody well that Ashley never smoked. He never had. He was inclined to health freakishness in an old-fashioned Gaylord Hauser way. He had eaten yoghurt when no one knew what it was. Inclined towards organic foods before anyone used the word. He certainly never smoked.

'Just shows how little you really know about me,' said Ashley. He lit a full strength Marlboro and inhaled.

'I suppose,' said Tudor.

'So what exactly did Lorraine tell you?'

'Only that you and she had been having a relationship. That

she was very fond of you. I was pleased. She seemed very nice.'

'She had no right.' Ashley sucked hard on the cigarette. 'She had absolutely no business telling you about us. Not,' he corrected himself quickly, 'that there was anything to tell. But if there was she shouldn't have said anything. It's a betrayal.'

'OK,' said Tudor, 'I'm sorry. It's none of my business. But I'm sorry she's dead.'

'No it's not,' said Ashley, bitterly. 'Absolutely none of your business. And I'm sorry too. What makes you think I wouldn't be? Just because you and I spend our lives up to our elbows in sudden death doesn't mean to say that we aren't distressed by the real thing when it happens to us. Or to people we know. I don't know what's happened to you but I've not been desensitized. Prick me and I bleed.'

'Quite.'

Ashley broke another uncomfortable silence by stubbing out his cigarette and saying, 'So I apologize. Accepted?'

'Of course,' said Tudor, not meaning it. 'But I'm still confused. What were all those e-mails about? I don't get it.'

'What e-mails, dear boy? I don't know what you're talking about.'

'The ones you sent, asking me to enter the mulled wine competition.'

Ashley laughed a harsh, mirthless bark of a laugh and Basil whined in sympathy.

'I don't know what you're talking about. Honest injun.' Ashley put a hand on his heart.

'Oh, come on.' This time Tudor did take a sizeable glug of shiraz. 'Don't be silly. You sent me several e-mails telling me to enter the competition and directing me towards your special ingredients which were in your desk drawer just as you said. I think you owe me an explanation.'

Ashley stared at him.

'Are you serious?'

'Never more so.'

'Even supposing you did get e-mail messages to that effect, whatever makes you think they came from me?'

'Are you calling me a liar?' Tudor was uncomfortably aware of losing his cool. Not at all what he intended.

'Oh Tudor, old friend,' Ashley sighed, 'surely you know me better than that? After all these years . . . where is trust? Where is comradeship? We go back a long way, you and I. Surely that counts for something?'

'You're suggesting that I've invented a story about your sending me e-mails.'

Ashley sighed and exhaled cigarette smoke.

'Don't be silly. I'm simply suggesting that you may have misread some signals. You thought you were getting e-mails from me but you were mistaken.'

Tudor frowned.

'What exactly do you mean?'

'Look,' said Ashley, 'we're neither of us enormously computer-literate. No one older than about twelve really is. Not unless they're Bill Gates or a seriously committed anorak.'

Ashley was still frowning.

'Go on,' he said, 'I get by with computers. I've passed my driving test: I'm as good on my laptop as I am with my car. Keyboard, dashboard . . . all the same to me.'

'You know perfectly well you'd be pushed to change a wheel let alone a faulty radiator or a rear axle. It's the same with the computer.'

'So?'

'So you couldn't detect a computer fraud in a month of Sundays. All you can really do is basic word-processing, send and receive e-mail and access information through sites like Google. How do you know it was me who sent those messages.'

'They sounded like you. And they were signed by you.'

'Well any half-baked forger would make sure the text sounded tolerably like me. And you can forge an electronic signature as easily as a handwritten one. How did you know it was my signature?'

Tudor was embarrassed. It was true. He was computer literate by the standards of his profession and according to his needs. But in real terms he was doing little more than talk pidgin.

'Well, first, the messages were signed by you. Second, the instructions about where to find the ingredients for the mull turned out to be accurate. And thirdly the electronic stuff was yours.'

'You mean it said the message had been sent by Ashley@unihav.com.au?'

'Absolutely.'

'And you think that constitutes proof?'

'Well . . .' Tudor recognized that he had been gullible. It was not just that he was a relative novice when it came to technology, it was also that this whole business of trust and friendship had fogged his natural scepticism. If it had been someone trying to sell him double-glazing or life insurance he wouldn't have believed.

Nevertheless . . .

'But why in God's name would anyone want to do that? Forge your signature on idiotic e-mails about the St Petroc's mulled wine competition?'

'That,' said Ashley, betraying his age, 'is the sixty-four thousand dollar question. Who wishes me harm? Do I have any enemies?'

Tudor remembered Jazz Trethewey's confession and the rivalry for the Dame's job. He took a risk.

'Jazz Trethewey suggested that you'd staged this vanishing trick simply to take me down a peg. That you'd decided I was a pompous Pom, an arrogant English bastard and this was your way of deflating me.'

Ashley stubbed out another cigarette and poured more Rymills.

'Did she just? Well, that's not exactly an act of friendship.'

'Are you suggesting that Jazz Trethewey sent the e-mails?'

'She doesn't like me. We have conflicting ambitions in certain areas. She's gay, of course, which complicates matters. And it would have been a doddle for her to send e-mails in my name. The university system is completely insecure. Any half-baked hacker could turn it to their advantage but it would help if you were part of it already.'

'I don't get it,' he said eventually. 'But are you saying that you definitely didn't send those e-mails?'

'Scout's honour old bean.'

'Shit,' said Tudor uncharacteristically. A week or so ago he would have accepted Ashley's anachronistic Baden-Powell assertion without a qualm. Now he had plenty of qualms but he was also hopelessly uncertain and disoriented.

'Do you think it was an accident?' he asked.

'What?'

'Lorraine Montagu's death?'

'It sounds like it. What else are you suggesting?'

'Well,' Tudor tried to rally, 'suppose she was poisoned. Suppose she drank my – our – mulled wine first – and that there was something in it which killed her. That there was a poison in the ingredients which I had been instructed to use by those e-mail messages. So whoever sent the e-mails committed murder by proxy.'

Ashley stared at his old friend over the top of his glass.

'You've been reading too many books,' he said, eventually. 'That's pure Father Brown.'

CHAPTER TWENTY-FOUR

Greg Sanders' office was as plain and neat as any Tudor had ever encountered. It contained a desk, two filing cabinets, a table with half-a-dozen chairs round it. There were no pictures on the walls. On the desk there was a laptop computer on to which, Tudor guessed, all the files from the cabinets would long ago have been transferred. The only deviation from clear, spare lines in not particularly varied shades of grey was an unusually large window looking out across Hobart City to the slopes of the Wurlitzer.

Today the view from the window was as grey as the room itself. It was a louring, drizzly day which drained all colour from the townscape and the mountain slopes. The summit itself was shrouded in a swirl of cloud.

The mood of the meeting was as subdued and monotone as the room and the view. It was Tudor's idea but the policeman had acquiesced with alacrity. They both had things to tell each other.

'You don't mind if Karen sits in on this?'

DCI Sanders nodded at WPC White who was looking pert, pretty and uniformed. Though phrased as a question it was actually a statement of fact. 'You don't mind if Karen sits in on this because I need a witness. If you say you mind you'll be overruled and although I'm not actually arresting you on a charge of anything and although you have come voluntarily and of your own accord I can, under Tasmanian law, detain you for just about as long as I like as a material witness in a case of sudden and hitherto unexplained death. This may or may not be Tasmanian law, but even though you are a world authority on criminal affairs this is such an out of the way place that I very much doubt whether you know that much about Tasmanian law and even if you do I shall produce any number of loopholes and precedents with which to confuse you. In any case you are anxious to assist the police in their enquiries, are you not?'

Sanders, naturally, said none of these things. They were best left unsaid and were so comprehensively understood by all three present that there was no need. Nonetheless the unsaid sentences hung in the air as tangible and enervating as the grey walls, carpet, fixtures and fittings within and the grey mist without.

'Fine,' said Tudor smiling and nodding. 'Fine, that's absolutely fine with me.'

'You don't mind if Karen takes a note,' said Sanders. Again a statement not a question and then, as if he had read Tudor's mind, Sanders said, 'Karen has immaculate shorthand and I have an old-fashioned aversion to tape recorders. More trouble than they're worth. Unreliable too. We may seem old-fashioned down here but in some respects the old and tested are, well, old and tested.'

Tudor smiled and nodded. He had some sympathy with this view.

Sanders was seated at the desk, Karen and Tudor at the table. The atmosphere was curiously ambivalent, not formal nor informal, not friendly nor cold. It wasn't even neutral enough to be neutral.

'Before you tell us why you wanted to talk to us,' said Greg, 'I should tell you that we've had the first reports of the autopsy and she was pregnant.'

Tudor found, to his surprise, that he was not surprised.

He said nothing.

'Somewhere between six and eight weeks we think,' he continued, answering the question Tudor had not asked.

'And you're assuming it was Ashley's?' said Tudor. Another statement masquerading as a question.

'I don't make assumptions while I'm waiting for proof positive. DNA testing will tell us for certain.'

'But the only DNA samples you'll take will be from Professor Carpenter?' Yet another faux-question.

Sanders nodded. 'We have the same presumption of innocence until proven guilty that you do in the UK,' he said. 'So even while I might harbour a suspicion I would never allow it to become an assumption until it was properly tested.'

Tudor nodded in turn. Fair enough. If the dead woman had been carrying Ashley's child it proved nothing beyond the fact that he was the father. Did it give him a motive for murder? Possibly. But just as possibly the reverse. What kind of man would murder his own unborn child? Didn't bear thinking about. You couldn't be sane, surely? Tudor had always had enormous difficulty with legal definitions of insanity. It seemed to him that some crimes were so barbaric and disgusting that their commission alone was evidence of insanity. But he knew this wasn't the case.

'What about cause of death?' he asked. 'Are we any further on?'

DCI Sanders said nothing for a while. Finally he seemed to make up his mind.

'You put me in a very difficult position,' he said. Then, looking across at the girl, he said, 'This had better be off the record Karen.' Outside, the whole of the mountain had vanished in mist and cloud and a thin rain was sliding into the window and running down the glass. They needed the strip lighting.

'Technically, I need hardly say, I shouldn't be confiding in you at all. On the other hand you have an international reputation as an expert in criminal affairs and especially criminal history in fact and fiction. I know and respect your work and it would be stupid of me not to avail myself of your assistance.' He seemed to be partly thinking out loud. 'Even if I can only do so informally and certainly without telling my bosses. As far as they are concerned a large part of these conversations have not taken place. Is that a problem?'

'Not in the least,' said Tudor. 'I'm grateful for your confidence.'

'Very well,' said Sanders. 'On that basis I can tell you that the pathologist hasn't come up with anything positive. On the other hand, the negatives are already pointing in a particular direction.'

Tudor wished he wouldn't speak in riddles but put it down to genuine confusion. He didn't blame him for that. He was confused too.

'Lorraine Montagu was asthmatic,' said Sanders, 'which meant that she occasionally suffered breathing difficulties. These were sometimes severe enough to be described as "attacks" and she had an inhaler prescribed by her doctor. She used it from time to time to ease discomfort and make her breathing easier, but it was never designed or used as a lifesaver. Her condition wasn't regarded as life-threatening.'

'Could the doctor have been wrong?' In Tudor's experience medical misdiagnosis was as common as not.

'You know as well as I do that doctors can make mistakes,' said Sanders, 'but in this case it seems unlikely. Montagu's doctor was a top woman. *Is* a top woman. She and the pathologist both agree that death was unlikely to have been caused by a more than usually severe attack of her asthma.'

'But it's possible?'

'Everything's possible. But it's improbable. What is definite is that there was no physical obstruction. She didn't choke on a fish bone. Or its equivalent.'

'So your people are suggesting that her asphyxia was caused by something in what she drank which triggered her condition. And because, according to Sammy, she only drank from my concoction it would have to be one of the ingredients in my brew.'

'Got it in one.'

'But it can't have been a poison in the conventional sense or everyone would have choked to death.'

'I'm with you,' said Sanders. Karen was scribbling frantically, her tongue touching her teeth as she concentrated.

'So there was something in my brew which killed her?'

'Mmmmhuh.'

This was agreement.

'Which either means it was a terrible mistake, or someone deliberately introduced a killer element into the drink.'

'Well, excuse me.' Sanders was very serious. 'But the only person who could have introduced such a killer element was you yourself. The system was foolproof.'

'Except for Sammy,' said Tudor.

'Except, possibly, for Sammy. But it would have been tricky. He was in full view of all the competing parties. You, on the other hand, were able to mix your drink in private without being seen.'

'Look,' said Tudor, realizing as he said it that his position was extremely weak, 'It's not as simple as that.'

'How not? It seems horribly straightforward to me.'

Tudor swallowed hard and told him the story of the e-mails. It took time and he didn't enjoy it.

When he had finished there was a long and awkward silence punctuated only by a few felt-tip-pen strokes from WPC White.

'What do you think, Karen?' asked the DCI eventually.

She sucked on her pen and finally said, 'It's so odd I guess I think it's likely true.'

'Why didn't you tell me this before?'

'To be honest, you never seemed that interested in Ashley's disappearance, if that's how we're going to describe it. It's only since Lorraine died that it seems particularly important. Until then it could hardly have been more trivial. Just some menopausal failed academic playing silly buggers.'

'Is that what you really think?'

'I don't know what I really think.' Tudor spoke more sharply than he intended. Not for the first time he wished he had more control over the impression he created. Still, it was true. He was confused. Hopelessly so.He felt almost as if he'd found his wife in bed with his best friend.

'If we take what you say at face value then you're telling me that Ashley Carpenter instructed you to concoct a lethal cocktail in order to kill his pregnant girlfriend.'

Long silence.

'I suppose if you put it like that, then yes.'

'How would you put it?'

'I don't know. Much the same if I were in your shoes. But I'm not. We're talking about my oldest friend here.'

'Can you prove that these e-mails were sent by Carpenter?'

'No. I don't think so. That's what he was saying earlier. He denies he sent them and says we can't prove it. Even if it's true.'

Sanders sunk his head in his hands and came up grimacing.

'God, I hate this modern technology,' he said. 'Have you kept the messages?'

'Yes.'

'So we can give them to some computer nerd to hack around with?'

'For what it's worth.'

'You didn't know Lorraine Montagu until you set foot in Tasmania, did you?' Sanders looked as if he liked this idea.

'Of course not.'

'Would be neat,' said Sanders, 'if she were someone from your past. Someone you wanted to kill. Someone who had done you wrong in an earlier life.'

'Neat, but not the truth,' said Tudor. 'Life and death are like that as we both well know. Messy businesses, both.'

'I'm inclined to believe you,' said the DCI eventually. 'Gut instinct. Respect for your reputation. It's not a professional way of proceeding. My bosses wouldn't sympathize. Sackable offence.' He grinned.

Tudor grinned back. 'Thanks a bunch,' he said. He was about to add something about trust and the heart being mightier than reason and the head, but then he thought of his relationship with Ashley and remained silent. His gut instincts hadn't done him a lot of good recently.

'No,' said Sanders, 'I'm not inclined to accuse you of murder and I have to wait for the next stage of the autopsy before I can be sure it *was* murder. If Watson says death was accidental or even due to unknown causes then I'll close the file.'

'Watson?'

'Government pathologist. Very good.'

Sanders stared at his laptop as if willing it to disgorge relevant secrets. His screen saver was the five ages of Rembrandt. Self-portraits of the painter from dashing youth to seedy dotage. They were daily reminders of the transitory nature of life and also of a hinterland, a world beyond the stark business of criminal detection. He would have liked to have been an artist or even an academic. He envied his guest.

'To be frank,' he said, 'I'm inclined to think that it's murder and I'm inclined to think that it was master-minded by Professor Carpenter who set it up but made you the unwitting instrument.'

'Not a very sharp instrument,' said Tudor. 'Positively blunt, in fact. I mean I could see that the whole business was eccentric and even batty, but it never occurred to me that I was being made to kill someone.'

'Isn't it all a bit too straightforward?'

This from Karen White.

'Straightforward?' The two men were incredulous.

'It seems positively byzantine to me,' said Tudor. 'What are you getting at?'

'I'm sorry,' said Karen, 'it's a hunch again. Very unprofessional I know. It's just that there are two aspects of the business which bother me. One is that there's something feminine about it all. Don't ask me what or how, but this doesn't strike me as an entirely masculine crime. If it *is* a crime. And also I feel there's something conspiratorial about the whole place.'

'You mean St Petroc's?'

'Yes,' she said. 'I know I'm an outsider and I know it's a closed community and I understand about how nutty professors can be, but even so there's something about the college which is sort of spooky. I just wonder if it wasn't in everyone's interests to have Lorraine Montagu dead. After all she was the only half-way normal person there and because of her skeleton she knew where the skeletons were buried.'

The first few bars of 'Click Go the Shears' suddenly shrilled from Sanders' jacket pocket. He swore and pulled out a mobile phone.

'This is he,' he said, then listened. From time to time he nodded. Occasionally he grunted rather as if he had taken something on board and was allowing the speaker to move on to the next hurdle. Once or twice he said, 'Are you sure?' Just once he whistled with what appeared to be astonishment. Finally he said, 'Thanks Arthur. Great work. Be in touch. Love to Sybil.'

Then he turned to Tudor.

'Looks like murder,' he said. 'That was Watson. I told you he was good. It could have taken him weeks if he'd gone by the book and run all the tests according to the rules but luckily he played a hunch.'

'A honey hunch,' said Tudor.

Sanders looked at him with surprise mingled with suspicion.

'What makes you say that?'

Tudor shrugged.

'I'd read it somewhere. I wondered about wattles and all those other antipodean bush ingredients, but I kept coming back to the Royal Jelly. It's rare as dodoes though, isn't it?'

'That's what Watson said. He's never seen a case before but he'd read a paper in some bee-keeping journal or other. Watson reads like no one I've ever met. Anyway it's a one in a million. She must have been allergic to honey and in the pure concentrate form of Royal Jelly that drink would have been lethal. No antidote. Certain death in seconds. She hadn't a hope. And with all those other pungent additives knocking around she'd never have suspected a thing. The only thing that Royal Jelly transmitted was sweetness. No real taste. Just sweetness.'

'Sweet, sweet, sweet poison,' said Tudor, smiling softly.

'Sorry?' said Sanders.

'Shakespeare,' said Tudor, '*King John*. Not one of the better plays. It was the OUDS major our first summer.'

'Eh?'

'The Drama Society's production at Oxford. I seem to remember Ashley was involved in some way. A stagehand perhaps. We had a friend who played Lady Faulconbridge. She had an illicit affair with Richard Coeur de Lion. "By long and vehement suit I was seduc'd . . . to make room for him in my husband's bed." '

He saw that the other two were looking at him strangely.

'Sorry,' he said. 'All a long time ago. It doesn't have anything to do with anything. Sweet poison. You never think of death as "sweet" do you?'

CHAPTER TWENTY-FIVE

Tudor remembered a story by R. Austin Freeman who had been medical officer at Holloway Prison and a doctor at the Middlesex Hospital in the 1920s. Famous in his day. 'It appears to be a watery solution of some kind,' one of his detectives had said, on discovering a corpse with a bottle in one hand, 'but I can't give it a name. Where is the cork?'

Tudor had composed a celebrated lecture on *Poisons unknown to medical science* which he subtitled, *I can't give it a name. Where is the cork?*

The phrase now crept into his brain and refused to be dislodged. It was like an advertising jingle or one of those naff Christmas top-of-the-pops. Catchy in a cheap, irritating way which stayed with him like the after-taste of smoked fish. 'A watery solution of some kind.' Well, it was a vinous solution of some kind, and it was sweetened with Royal Jelly. Perfectly innocuous except for one person in, what? a hundred thousand, a million, a billion, a trillion? Who knew, who cared? It was what made statistics so meaningless. Lies, damned lies and stats. What did it matter to Lorraine Montagu that she was one in a million, a billion, or a trillion? As far as she was concerned she was one in one. Dead. Bad luck. Oh, Hobart is as safe as houses. Tasmania has one of the lowest crime rates in the world. Murder? Here? Not a prayer. But there was just that infinitessimal chance of sudden death. And Lorraine was the person to whom it happened. The one who won the jackpot. Well played, Lorraine. *I can't give it a name. Where is the cork?* Allergic to honey? Amazing! Give her the money!

Tudor kicked an empty Diet-Coke can into the gutter. This was supposed to have been an idyllic sabbatical semester. Instead this. But what *was* this? The betrayal of an old friend? The murder of the friend's mistress? A murder in which he himself was the executioner? Oh, give me a break. These things don't happen to ordinary blameless people, but yes, they do just that and that is what his whole academic life had taught him. That sudden, random horror lights on the least likely person at the least likely moment. One of God's private jokes. God must laugh a lot.

He was sufficiently self-aware to realize that he was at the end of his tether, wherever that might be.

As he turned into St Petroc's a slight figure emerged from the shadows. The person seemed to have been waiting for him.

'Doctor Cornwall!'

It was little Brad Davey, the Principal's assistant.

'Can I get you a coffee?' he asked.

Tudor had heard more enticing opening gambits. He didn't feel much like a coffee and he didn't feel much like Brad Davey, but he was a guest in a strange place in a strange country. It would be churlish to refuse. He also presumed that Brad had something more interesting on offer than coffee. Or thought he had. In a college which seemed to suffer from an excess of Character with a capital 'c' Brad Davey was the one member who seemed intent on restoring some sense of balance.

'That would be nice.'

'I have some interesting Colombian,' Davey said, 'if you like it strong.'

They walked across the quad and upstairs to Davey's apartment where it turned out that he was some sort of coffee freak. He had a commercial-sized Gaggia espresso machine and cups from Illy of Trieste. His room was decorated with coffee advertisements, stills from the Gold Blend commercials, and a shot of Humphrey Bogart in a trench coat and a snappy fedora hat holding what was presumably a coffee cup.

'Keen on coffee?' said Tudor, gazing round the otherwise unexceptional room with surprise.

'It's an interest of mine. People should have an interest. Mine's coffee.'

Tudor wondered whether to revise his thoughts on Davey's lack of character and decided against it.

'Jazz Trethewey says she tried to apologize but you didn't seem to take in what she was saying.'

'Oh. Well, I had other things on my mind. Things seem to have moved on.'

'That's right.' He fiddled with levers on the coffee machine which hissed obligingly. Tudor decided not to talk over the sibilant sounds and waited until Brad handed him a small quantity of very strong coffee in a very small Illy mug.

'It seemed a neat idea at the time.'

Tudor frowned.

'How do you mean exactly?'

'Ashley's disappearing trick. OK, he said, we've got this English guy coming as a visiting fellow and he's supposed to be an authority on crime and mysteries and all that, so let's see what he does when he gets caught up in a real mystery. So he staged this disappearance and we were all supposed to react as if it were no big deal especially. And he asked me to send you these e-mails just to stir the pot. That's what he said "Just to stir the pot".'

'E-mails?' said Tudor. 'He got you to send me e-mails?'

'Yup. "To stir the pot".' Davey stirred his coffee vigorously as if to emphasize what he was saying.

'Pretending that they came from him?'

'Yup. He gave me all the passwords and that. He thought it would make you even more confused.'

'Well, he got that right,' said Tudor. 'And they included the instructions on making a mull for the college competition?'

The principal's deputy looked embarrassed if not quite ashamed.

'He said it would make you even more confused. Also he had some idea it would remind you of when you were students. Said you used to drink that sort of stuff at Christmas.'

'Perhaps so,' said Tudor.

'Wassail,' said Brad. ' "Here we go a wassailing" was what he said. I didn't know the word.'

'No,' said Tudor. 'Did he write down what you were to say?'

'No,' said Brad. 'I asked him but he wouldn't. He was very insistent. Said the less evidence we left lying around the more difficult it would be for you to solve the puzzle.'

'So it's your word against his?'

'He told Jazz and Tasman. Maybe Sammy. Not Dame Edith. He didn't think Dame Edith would see the funny side of it.'

'Nor Lorraine?'

'I don't think so. Just the Fellows. He seemed to think that was enough.'

'And did all three of you know about the e-mails?'

'No, he said it was a little secret between the two of us. He treated the whole thing like a game.'

'An academic exercise?'

'Yeah. But . . .' Brad hesitated. 'I got the impression he was keen to see you screw up.'

'In what way?'

'Well, it was more than just setting you a problem. It was a sort of get-even thing. Like he really wanted you to come out looking stupid. He made out you were, well, you know, stuck up, arrogant, needed taking down a bit.'

'He didn't say that we were old friends?'

'Yeah. He said that.'

'Not a specially friendly thing to do, would you say?'

The coffee was extraordinarily good. The machine and its steam engine noise was just about justified.

Brad gave the impression he hadn't previously considered this.

'Suppose not. But he gave the impression that there was some sort of, you know, academic seriousness about it all. Also that you deserved to be made to look dumb.He didn't make you sound very nice. Sorry.We didn't know any better.'

'Thanks. Did you keep copies of the messages?'

'No. But they'll be there somewhere in the memory. You can always find things if you want to even if you think you've got rid of them.'

'That's not what happens when I lose a file by mistake.' Tudor grimaced. 'I can never retrieve them. But I think you're right. The experts say they can always find stuff, given time.'

He frowned into the dregs of his coffee, declined a second helping and pondered. Ashley had meant the e-mails to confuse him, but on balance Ashley meant to convince Tudor that they were really coming from him. In this he had succeeded. He had also banked on Tudor carrying out his instructions. And why not? They seemed merely eccentric and batty in a mad-donnish way. Why shouldn't he do as he was told. And ultimately, if and when the matter became public, Ashley would deny all knowledge of them. As he had already started to do. And whatever anyone believed it would be next to impossible to prove anything. That was the trouble with the electronic, digital age. Everything was forgeable. No one believed the old saw about the camera never lying. And it was the same with the computer. The opportunities for indecipherable deceit were incalculable.

'Why are you telling me this? And why should I believe you?'

Brad seemed startled by these questions.

After a while he said, 'I guess we all feel it's gone beyond a joke. I don't know what Lorraine's death has to do with it all but it makes it serious. And, if you'll pardon me saying it, you don't seem to be quite the sort of guy Ashley told us you were.'

'I suppose I should find that flattering.'

'What Ashley told us in the first place wasn't flattering,' said Brad. 'Not one bit. He made you seem like a real monster.'

'Charming,' said Tudor. 'I've always spoken very highly of him.'

This, though delivered in a mock jocular fashion, was perfectly true. Tudor kept puzzling over Ashley's unexpected outburst about Miranda. There had seemed genuine vicious resentment there. Were there other resentments too? It was true for reasons of geography as much as anything that Tudor was better known than Ashley. He wrote for better known newspapers, got on extra-terrestrial TV more frequently. But he was closer to major newspaper offices and TV studios so naturally he got more exposure. Also his generalist approach to criminal studies was, well, sexier than Ashley's more technically based forensic interests. If you wanted a quasi-academic review of a new movie of Dostoevsky or a think piece on the death penalty, then Tudor was your man. Ashley was the bee's knees on genetic fingerprinting. You paid your money and you took your choice. Being in such a different time zone from London and New York didn't help Ashley in this respect either. But they were friends, weren't they? Maybe that made it worse whatever 'it' was.

'Are you sure?' he asked.

'It's not something I'd make up,' said Brad. 'It was strange though. I'd never thought of Professor Carpenter as, you know, like . . . vindictive. He always seemed easy-going, friendly. Not like him to be so full of . . . well, hatred isn't too strong a word.'

Tudor ran a hand through his hair. He didn't get it. Could Brad be making it up? He didn't have him down as an inventive person. Or not until he'd discovered the coffee mania. But why should he make up something like this?

'So, what's your explanation?'

'I don't have an explanation.'

'Did you like Lorraine?'

He shrugged.

'I had no problem with Lorraine. Some people thought she knew too much. Was too close to Dame Edith. She was always nice to me.'

'Do you think what happened to her was an accident?'

'Why? Wasn't it?'

A shade too quick, thought Tudor. Of course, he suspected there was more to Lorraine's death than an accident. So would the others. They must have been talking. It would have been weird if they hadn't.

'What would you say,' Tudor was choosing his words with care, 'what would you say if you discovered that between us we'd murdered Lorraine Montagu?'

'I'd say you'd have to be joking. In bad taste.'

Tudor looked at him carefully. He was telling the truth. He had no idea.

'You didn't know that Lorraine suffered from some potentially deadly allergies?'

'I knew she had an asthma problem. We all knew that.She had one of those little puffers. But it seemed quite manageable.'

'Well.' There didn't seem any harm in spelling it out. 'Suppose she did have an allergy. Suppose Ashley Carpenter knew what that allergy was. Suppose he persuaded you to persuade me to administer a substance to which she was fatally allergic.'

'It's a lot of "supposes",' said Brad. 'But supposing the suppositions are correct then I guess it could make both of us murderers.'

'I don't know what local law says.' Tudor looked thoughtful, 'but I have a feeling we could both be in trouble unless we're very careful. Is there anything else you haven't told me? Because if there is then now's your chance. Leave it any longer and there may not be another.'

'I'm going to make more coffee,' said Brad, 'while I think about it.'

CHAPTER TWENTY-SIX

Doctor Tudor Cornwall was blessed with an almost photographic memory for odd details. At school and university he had suffered in comparison with some rivals whose memory was perfect. In those days of learning by rote, the ability to spout great chunks of *Othello* or French irregular verbs after a single sighting was priceless. Tudor had never possessed this gift and though it paid handsome dividends in three-hour exams without source-books or other cribs, he had doubts about its efficacy in the longer game of life itself.

He realized very early, however, that those blessed with this all-embracing blanket recall often had difficulty in distinguishing wood from trees. In fact *not* remembering everything could be turned to his advantage. If you only remembered a few things you had to be selective; you learned to prioritize. He also learned that when it came to the detection of crime and deduction in matters criminal, it was very often the tiny things that made the difference – the dog that did not bark in the night, the speck of mud on the trouser turn-up, the tell-tale give-away of a dropped aitch or glottal stop too far. Tudor therefore acquired the habit of memorizing what to others often seemed trivial but in his experience frequently proved crucial.

And so it happened this time. It was the odd, quirky detail that he had noticed and squirelled away. At the time it had seemed a matter of no moment but with the passage of time, as so often happened, it was the one clue which might wrap the case up. 'Ignore the obvious,' he told his students, 'and observe the igniter.' 'Igniter' was a technical term, he told them, but not being a scientist himself, he was content to know simply that it meant 'a person or thing who ignites.' He thought of the igniter as the unsuspected catalyst, the hidden key, the unexpected answer, the missing piece of the jigsaw. This time he had observed an igniter, filed it away and committed it to the memory.

He did not want to run the risk of his telephone conversation being overheard. He was becoming paranoid about such things, his conspiracy theory working overtime. So he took his mobile into the nearby park and called international enquiries to ask for the number of Beaubridge Friary in Oxfordshire. A few minutes later he was talking to their Brother Barnabas. The community was, it turned out, fully computerized. All their records, including mail-order sales were on file. If Dr Cornwall cared to call back in an hour's time, Brother Barnabas would have been able to run a check and produce the information he wanted. Not a problem, and while he was on the phone might he say how much he admired Dr Cornwall's essay on *Crime and the Clergy* in the *Tablet*? Tudor effused in return. He never ceased to be amazed by crime fans.

He went back to his room to collect his thoughts, but before he got there he had an idea, changed tack and went to see the Principal.

Dame Edith was working on papers. Tudor gained the impression that it was therapy rather than real life, rather like her painting of the echidna. He had a sense of pieces of paper being shuffled from one pile to another in a sort of academic-bureaucratic game of patience or solitaire. After an hour or so, the papers would be in exactly the order in which they started out but the Principal's nerves would have been soothed and her feathers unruffled.

'I need your help,' he said.

'Such is life,' she said, putting down her fountain pen and adjusting a green eyeshade like a golfer's visor which, presumably, was protecting her eyes from the glare of the electric light.

'I want an address for a student.'

'Most students live on campus,' she said.

'This one is in digs. Or has an apartment. Something. It might be in addition to a room on campus. It might be illegal, but if Lorraine was as omniscient as I sense she was then it'll show up in her files.'

'I have a copy of most of her electronic material,' said the Dame. 'Don't be fooled into thinking that my extreme age is any sort of barrier to my technological competence.'

She smiled. Her computer was on a side table.

'Who do you want?'

'Elizabeth Burney.'

'Oh dear. She's in college though, surely?'

'Let's see.'

The Dame pressed some buttons, moved her mouse around a foam rubber map of Australia and frowned.

'There's an address downtown. Very irregular but everything about that girl is irregular.

'Why do you need to know?'

Tudor swallowed hard. Keeping secrets hadn't done him much good so far.

'When Ashley disappeared he's supposed to have sheltered in some mountain hut. I don't think he did.'

'Why not?'

'Various reasons,' said Tudor, 'including not least what I've sensed are Ashley's increasingly sybaritic tastes and inclinations. I don't see him chilling out in some primitive shack with no central heating, hot shower, breakfast in bed and all that.

But the clincher's Basil.'

'Ashley's dog?'

'Exactly.'

'Perhaps you could explain?'

'Ashley was devoted to the dog. If he'd been in some rural fastness he'd have kept the dog for company and no reason why not. If he abandoned the dog he did it because whatever retreat he had actually found wasn't dog-friendly. Like a small apartment in a high-rise building downtown.'

'Does Elizabeth Burney's downtown address fit that description?'

'It could,' said the Dame wearily. She read it out and Tudor made a note.

'What do you think?' she asked, sounding plaintive and tired.

'I think little Miss Burney is a manipulative little minx and that Ashley is going through a particularly traumatic male menopause. Beyond that I'm not sure.'

'So what exactly are you going to do?'

'Something,' said Tudor. 'I've spent too long in not very masterly inactivity. Actually I'm going to phone a cab, go round and have a word with little Miss Burney.'

The Dame sighed.

'I suppose you know what you're doing,' she said. 'My understanding was that you were an academic not action man. Academics are supposed to spend their time in quiet and serene contemplation.'

'I couldn't agree more,' said Tudor, 'But needs must.'

She rang for a cab and the company switchboard said a car would be at the front gate in five minutes. Tudor thanked the old girl. He felt sorry for her. She obviously craved serenity and quiet. Jobs like hers were supposed to be gentle retirement posts, and while the modern world imposed innovative burdens to do with red tape and fund-raising there was nothing which said that the heads of university colleges had to deal with sudden death and professors who staged fake disappearances, tried to bamboozle Visiting Fellows and generally cause confusion and dissent.

The cab driver was inclined to be talkative, but Tudor's grunts and monosyllables seemed to shut him up. He wondered if it was time to ring Brother Barnabas, his new friend at Beaubridge Friary, but he decided not to chance it but leave it till after he had investigated Miss Burney's town residence.

The building was high rise by Hobart standards which Tudor put at around fifteen storeys max. The front doors were locked but unattended. This was not the sort of building which boasted a uniformed concierge or even a surly porter you could rouse from sleep. The individual apartments had entry-phones and 8b, presumably on the eighth floor, indicated that the occupant was E. Burney. He hesitated about buzzing, but reckoned he had no alternative. If she didn't let him in he'd talk to DCI Sanders and come back with a search warrant. Well, that was the theory. Back home in Casterbridge he knew the police well enough to be able to stretch a point on the few occasions he had cause to ask. He wasn't sure about Tasmania but he had hopes of Sanders.

He buzzed. There was a longish pause. Then a girl's voice came crackling down.

'Christ, you're late and now you've forgotten your key. God you're useless.'

Tudor smiled. It was time his luck turned. He said nothing but pushed the door open as Elizabeth Burney unlocked it from her eighth floor eyrie.

The hall was drab, featureless. A chained bicycle was propped against a wall. The paint was pale green and peeling. The floor was lino and curling at the corners like an old ham sandwich. A police poster appealed for help in finding a missing person, female, seventeen years old. The elevator was basic but gave every evidence of functioning so Tudor got in and pressed eight.

She was standing in the doorway of her flat wearing a man's shirt several sizes too large which came down to her knees and a pair of plastic flip-flops.

For a moment Tudor thought she was going to try slamming the door in his face.

'Shit!' she said, flatly. 'It's not you.'

'Sorry,' he said, not meaning it. 'Your man's obviously been detained. I'd say he had an increasing amount on his plate. May I come in.'

'Sure,' she said. 'Why not?'

She stood aside and shut the door behind him.

The place was small and had a transient feel.

'Mind if I use the loo?' he asked.

'Sure,' she said again, robotically. 'Why not?' Tudor wondered if she were high. She had a druggy look to her and at their previous encounters she had seemed positively sparky. Now she seemed spaced out.

The toilet was in the same room as the shower and wash basin and he found what he was looking for: a chunky male razor, shaving soap, two toothbrushes. Was it jumping to conclusions to guess that they belonged to Ashley? He supposed so. The place had the feel of a seedy hotel room, the sort of accommodation in which men might pitch up at short notice for short stays and where the provision of basic shaving and toothbrushing kit was a sensible precaution. They could be anybody's. Was Elizabeth Burney on the game? Just throwing the occasional trick? It was how some girls paid their way through college, especially if they had expensive habits. Tudor was only too well aware of this from his experiences back home at the good old Wessex Uni. No reason why things should be drastically different out here, down under. How on earth could someone like Ashley have got mixed up with a girl like Elizabeth? Don't ask. Happened all the time. It was a sad cliché.

All this clattered through his brain in the time it took to have a quick pee, take in his surroundings and flush the loo.

She was smoking a cigarette when he came out.

'Coffee?' she asked, 'Or a glass of red?'

He was coffeed out.

'Glass of red,' he said, 'provided it's not sparkling.'

She produced a half-empty bottle of something basic and poured two glasses.

'What's going on?' she asked. 'I don't like it.'

'You tell *me* what's going on,' he said. 'I know nothing. Nobody tells me anything at all. Worse than that there's been a deliberate attempt to make an idiot of me ever since I arrived here. Maybe before. And it's all orchestrated by your beloved Ashley Carpenter.'

She took a gulp of wine and made a derisive, dismissive noise which was half cough, half snort.

'Ashley is *not* beloved but he's a pushover and he could be useful. A girl needs all the help she can get in my situation. As a matter of fact, your friend Ashley is pretty disgusting. But that's a condition of most men at his time of life. You should know.'

She gave him a lip-curling look and blew cigarette smoke down her nose.

'He stayed here when he was staging his brilliantly amusing "disappearance?" ' said Ashley.

'Yeah,' she said, disdainfully. 'He really did fool himself he was going to rough it up on the mountain. In some ski-hut or other. No way. He made it as far as the building, took one look and got me to pick him up. Tough luck on Basil. He can't stay here. No pets allowed. And look at it. You couldn't have a dog in here. Especially a Basil!'

She sniggered.

'So Ashley was shacked up here with you all the time he was supposed to have vanished.'

'There's no law against it,' she said. 'And if you think he's making you look stupid, look at what I'm doing to him. He doesn't know where he is. One minute he's having sex with the Lolita of St Petroc's and the next he's being reported for harassment. Cool.'

Tudor almost felt sorry for his old friend.

'But what happened to Lorraine's not cool,' she said sharply. 'That's gross. Was it an accident? I don't like it. If it wasn't an accident I want out. I'll do most things but not if means someone getting hurt. Much less killed. That's not so funny. So I need to know: was it an accident? Or what?'

There was a noise off. Key in door. They both turned, Tudor stepping back out of sight so that when the newcomer entered he saw only Elizabeth.

'Hi, sweetie!' said Professor Carpenter. 'Sorry I'm late. Hard day at the office.'

Then as Tudor stepped out of the shadows he managed, with a barely perceptible pause to articulate a credibly unsurprised, 'Oh Tudor, old bean. Fancy seeing you here. I'd no idea you and Lizzie had become so intimate so quickly. You always were a fast worker, you old dog. Eh?! I take off more than my hat!'

CHAPTER TWENTY-SEVEN

There was another bottle of vinegary red in the cupboard and presently all three had a glass in hand. Ashley and the girl were smoking.

'Right,' said Tudor. 'Payback time.'

'I'm not sure I understand what's going on,' said Ashley.

'Do shut up,' said Elizabeth, 'and grow up. You're old enough to know when you've been found out.'

'Shut up yourself,' said Ashley petulantly. 'I'm telling you, I don't know what this is all about.'

Tudor pulled out his mobile.

'In a minute,' he said, 'I'm going to make a phone call which may just provide the missing link in this peculiar chain of events. The igniter. But first let me recap.'

He had their attention. The impending unexplained phone call intrigued both of them. Ashley seemed truculent. The girl subdued.

'I don't pretend to be happy about any of this,' said Tudor. 'I thought you asked me here because it would be enjoyable and relaxing and academically stimulating.'

'Oh do cut all that old boy Oxford crap,' said Ashley, nastily.

'You used to be an absolute sucker for old boy Oxford crap,' Tudor reminded him. With justice.

'Sucker's the *mot juste*, old bean,' said Ashley.

The girl gave Tudor a look which said that she'd had her doubts but that the Professor of Criminology had finally flipped.

'OK,' said Tudor. 'You set me up. I still don't properly understand why but you asked me out here in order to humiliate me. You staged a vanishing trick and challenged me to solve the problem. When I couldn't, you thought you'd use it as a stick to beat me with and demonstrate that I was no good at my job, couldn't tell a motive from an alibi, didn't know my Holmes from my Watson, thought DNA was the same as DIY and was just a bogus academic. Or words to that effect.'

'Very good, old boy,' said Ashley. 'Very good. First class in fact.'

'The trouble was,' Tudor ploughed on, 'that you weren't content with your rather feeble practical joke. You decided to dabble in a more serious sort of crime. You'd been having an affair with Lorraine Montagu and she was becoming more and more possessive and more and more demanding, wanted to settle down, wanted to marry, and then God help her, got pregnant.'

This looked like news to Elizabeth Burney. She stared at Ashley and shook her head.

'Arsehole,' she said.

'So,' continued Tudor, 'you decide that your mistress and your unborn child are better off out of the way, particularly as you have now embarked on a sordid little relationship with one of your students. A relationship which seems to have turned your head somewhat, just as relationships like this so often do when they concern dirty old men.'

He wished he didn't so often catch himself sounding prissy. The girl was right. He had a strong element of potential dirty-old-mannism himself. Just because he managed to keep it in check didn't give him a licence to sermonize sanctimoniously making himself out holier-than-Ashley.

'Now,' he continued, trying to push his voice into a neutral gear which wasn't what he felt, 'because of your intimacy with Lorraine Montagu you knew about her medical condition; you knew that she was mildly asthmatic; but you also knew that she suffered from an extremely rare allergy which meant she couldn't touch honey. Honey was bad enough, but in a concentrated form such as Royal Jelly it would be lethal. If Lorraine ingested even a small quantity of Royal Jelly she'd choke to death in a matter of seconds and there would be nothing anyone could do about it. No known antidote.

'But you can't take the risk of administering a fatal dose yourself so what do you do?'

He had their attention now all right. Much of this was obviously news to the girl. What was news to Ashley, however, was that the game was, if not over or up, at least tilting dangerously away from his initiative.

Neither of them said anything, so Tudor continued.

'So you persuade wretched little Brad Davey to send me some e-mails telling me to concoct your special recipe for mulled wine to enter in the annual St Petroc wassailling competition. Or whatever. They appear to be signed by you and they have enough message ID, content-transfer-encoding and other easily arranged electronic sender guff to persuade me that the message does indeed come from my old friend and that in the present admittedly perplexing circumstances, I might as well do as I'm being asked. After all, you are my friend, and what you ask seems, though mildly farcical, to be perfectly harmless.

'What I don't know and nor does little Brad, is that your mistress has this fatal allergy to one of the ingredients you've carefully stored in the drawer of your desk at St Petroc's.Which means that the Royal Jelly seems no more sinister to me than the wattle berry or kangaroo dung, or any of the other Waltzing Matilda bush tucker ingredients you've dreamed up. Nor to Brad.'

Ashley and the girl stayed silent.Ashley was looking at the floor, truculence suddenly evaporated. Elizabeth Burney stared at him with dawning horror.

'So come the fatal evening,' said Tudor, 'I've mixed my evil potion; taken it to the refectory; handed it over to Sammy who sets the whole thing in motion.Then, hey presto, Lorraine takes a mouthful, fails to detect the Royal Jelly whose flavour, such as it is, has been crowded out by all the exotic spices of the outback, and is departed this life in a matter of moments. And Ashley is far from the scene of the crime, innocent as the day is long.'

Ashley spoke. His voice had shrunk and gone strangely tinny.

'Even if any of this were true,' he said, 'you couldn't prove a word.'

'Ah,' said Tudor, 'because the instructions came from Brad and the mixing was done by me, and you'd deny all knowledge of everything. I wonder if you were going to claim that the whole business was a miserable accident, or whether you were going to try to pin a murder rap on me.' Tudor sighed. 'We'll never know, will we?'

'It's complete rubbish,' said Ashley, 'The sort of thing only a tenth-rate British academic could dream up.'

'It's not, is it, Ashley?' The girl looked at him piercingly. 'He's telling the truth. It's crazy but it's true.'

'Even if . . .' said Ashley. 'Even if there was a scintilla, an iota of truth in this whole idiotic concoction there is absolutely no way in the world that you could possibly prove a thing. A thing. Not a thing.' He shook his head with manic certainty.

'Now.' Tudor looked at his mobile as if it were the key which was about to unlock a wardrobe of skeletons and a cupboard of clues. 'That phone call,' he said. 'Time I rang the friary.' And he jabbed at the buttons, memorized like other apparent trivia by his eccentric brain.

'Brother Barnabas please,' he said, registering his audience's incomprehension, and then, after a momentary wait, 'Brother Barnabas. Tudor Cornwall again . . . you were going to check the records to see whether . . . yes, that's right, Tasmania . . . yes . . . oh, good . . . how very efficient . . . the 7th of last month . . . six weeks ago . . . and you sent them by courier . . . paid by Mastercard . . . uh huh . . . just one packet . . . I agree, it does seem a small order considering the delivery charges but I dare say he didn't need, well, never mind . . . and you can supply all the documentation? . . . Excellent . . . A favour? . . . The annual Friary dinner . . . St Francis's day next year . . . I'm sure that would be wonderful but could you possibly send me a formal letter at the university? . . . Yes, Casterbridge and the zip . . . oh, OK. Thank you, you've been most helpful And good morning to you too!'

He put the mobile back in his pocket and smiled wolfishly at Ashley.

'Charming fellow,' he said. 'Had you neatly logged into his system. Funny, isn't it? I was lecturing on Chesterton and Father Brown; talking about deceptive appearances; how Brown got away with murder – well, the antithesis of murder I suppose – by wearing a dog collar and looking simple. It's part of *Crime and the Clergy*. Well . . . I could go on but let's just say that Brother Barnabas is absolutely up to speed and he has your purchase of a small packet of Royal Jelly capsules meticulously logged and catalogued. No room for doubt. Chapter and verse all there.'

Tudor smiled at them both.

'So,' he said, 'what about that then?'

'Well what about it?' Ashley sounded belligerent but uncertain. 'So someone claiming to be me ordered a packet on Royal

Jelly capsules from some dinky monastery in Mother England. So bloody what?'

'So Lorraine Montagu was killed by ingesting Royal Jelly at a wine-tasting at St Petroc's College, Hobart, Tasmania. And a month or so earlier, her lover, Professor Ashley Carpenter, has ordered a small packet of Royal Jelly capsules. He is a Fellow of St Petroc's College, Hobart, Tasmania. I could go on. Need I?'

'Circumstantial,' said Ashley. 'You'd never stand it up in court.'

'I think most juries would convict,' said Tudor. 'I'd call Brother Barnabas. He'd make an excellent impression in the witness box. The forensics by which you set such store would be unassailable. Brad Davey—'

'Brad Davey would be in shreds,' said Ashley. 'Counsel for the Defence would have him for breakfast. Spit him out into the public gallery.'

'It's not a game,' said the girl, staring from one to another in disbelief.

'I wouldn't say that.' Ashley looked thoughtful. 'Do you remember an essay you wrote called *Would Lady Macbeth have got life?*'

'Yes.'

'That always got up my nose,' said Ashley. 'Professor Bingham was completely taken in by it.'

'Professor Brooke said the evidence of the Thane of Cawdor was tainted.'

They both smiled. The years rolled back.

'You're mad,' said Elizabeth Burney. 'Both of you.'

'I suppose,' said Ashley, 'that you expect me to say that it's a fair cop.'

'No.' Tudor thought for a moment. 'I'd never expect you to say anything like that. But I think you murdered Lorraine Montagu. And I think we've got the proof.'

'An awful lot hinges on your mad monk.'

'He's not mad and he's not a monk. He's a Franciscan friar. In any case you did it. You're admitting it. In front of a witness.'

Ashley poured them all another glass of rotgut.

'Even if I were to admit it I don't think Elizabeth would testify. Would you darling?'

The girl stared at the ceiling and pouted. 'I might,' she said, 'I might not. It would depend.'

'On what?' Tudor was genuinely intrigued.

'It would depend,' she said, 'on all kinds of things. The highest bid I suppose. But I don't have to decide in a hurry, do I?'

The two men looked at her. She seemed devastatingly old for her age.

'Now who's playing games?' asked Tudor.

She smirked.

'We're all playing games,' said Ashley. 'That's what this is all about. You, Tudor, you've been playing games ever since we first met. And you're good at it. Brilliant in fact. You've made a whole life out of death but you've never had a serious thought in your entire existence. People like you make a mockery of reality. Pain, grief, misery . . . they're all a joke as far as you're concerned. Human beings are just playing cards or counters on a board. Mister Bun the Baker. Professor Plum with the lead piping in the library.'

'I don't believe I'm hearing this,' said Tudor. 'You've just killed a woman you loved and you accuse me of playing games.'

Ashley exhaled. 'I remember P.D. James saying the perfect murder was pushing your husband over a cliff on a Sunday morning walk. Maybe she was right. Simple is best. I was too byzantine to use your sort of smart-arse word. Too baroque. I should just have pushed Lorraine through a window or under a car.'

'I don't get it,' said Tudor. 'Have you always hated me?

Underneath all that bonhomie and affability? Have you always seethed?'

Ashley smiled. 'No, no, dear boy. It's only a game.'

Tudor did not smile.

He let himself out.

CHAPTER TWENTY-EIGHT

The police received Dr Cornwall's report with only moderate enthusiasm. At university a favourite mark of Cornwall's had been alpha gamma on the grounds that it was as far removed from dull competence as it was possible to be. He encouraged his own students to aspire to something similar but he was careful to advise them that most employers much preferred pure beta. As far as he was concerned the average policeman came into the pure beta category. Its defenders would say that the mark suggested competence. Tudor preferred second-rate.

'The forensic evidence is clear,' said Sanders sitting at his soulless desk in his soulless office looking out on a view which had changed from monochrome to technicolour.

The sun was shining. The sky was blue.

'She was killed by an intake of Royal Jelly which was contained in the drink you mixed,' continued the DCI. 'You're telling me that you introduced the killing agent on instructions which purported to come from Professor Carpenter but actually emanated from Bradley Davey.'

Tudor had written a summary of what he had to say but Karen White was still doing her pert stenographer's act.

'That's about it,' he said.

'Sounds pretty thin when you express it like that,' said Sanders.

'You mean implausible,' said Tudor.

'I said thin,' said Sanders, 'and thin is what I mean.'

'I beg to differ.'

Sanders shrugged.

'I have to ask myself two questions,' he said. 'The first is do I believe your explanation? And the second is will a jury believe it? What do you think, Karen?'

The girl echoed her boss's gesture of defeat.

'I guess I believe Dr Cornwall because he's like, well, believable.'

'I'm sure he's pleased to hear it,' said Sanders drily.

He turned back to Cornwall. 'There's a lot going on here,' he said. 'Your friend Carpenter is getting pressured by Lorraine Montagu so he decides the easiest way is to kill her. Bit extreme, isn't it?'

'Happens all the time,' said Tudor. 'You know that as well as I do.'

'But Carpenter strikes everyone as sensible, mature, level-headed. The action's completely out of character.'

'Would have been completely out of character,' said Tudor. 'My view is that the character's changed.'

'Or the true character has only just revealed itself?'

'Or the true character has only just revealed itself.'

'You say he confessed in front of the girl.'

'More or less.'

'Well, which?' The policeman was becoming irritated. Tudor knew that donnishness had that effect. He had seen it before. All too often. 'Did he confess, or didn't he?'

'I'd testify that he did. My guess is that the girl won't. But the girl will make up her own mind and the truth won't come into it. At least I don't think it will. There may be some sort of perverted integrity lurking in there, but I wouldn't bank on it. Whatever she decides she'll be a lousy witness. Anything she says is going to sound thin and implausible.'

'I wouldn't bet on it,' said Sanders. 'She seems to have sorted you two out.'

A long silence ensued. WPC White had a scratchy pen.

'What do you think I should do?' Sanders asked, eventually.

'Bring him in for questioning.'

'Naturally.' Sanders sounded exasperated. 'He'll deny everything. Davey sent the instruction on his computer. You carried it out. His hands are clean.'

'But he bought the Royal Jelly. We can prove it.'

'Clever of you to remember the name of the manufacturer on the packet,' said Sanders, grudgingly. 'But he'll say it was a coincidence.'

'Pull the other one,' said Tudor. 'Murder suspect buys lethal substance and six weeks later his girlfriend swallows it and drops dead. That's not a coincidence. That's cause and effect.'

'Tell that to the judge.'

'It's not the judge that matters,' protested Tudor, 'it's the jury.'

'It all hinges on the girl,' said Karen White. 'Maybe I could talk to her.'

'Maybe,' said Sanders.

'He did it,' said Tudor. 'He killed her.'

'Actually no,' said Sanders, 'You did it. You mixed the lethal dose.'

'But I didn't have the first idea that Lorraine Montagu was allergic to honey for God's sake.'

'I've only your word for it.'

Tudor remembered what Ashley had said about playing games. This was what he and DCI Sanders were doing now. They both knew that Ashley had killed Lorraine Montagu but they were inventing false doubts in the interests of what? Fair play? Justice?

'Oh all right.' Sanders slammed his fist on the desk. A surprising gesture. He had seemed so cool. 'Karen's right. The girl's evidence is crucial but the odds are that no one is going to believe it. And if that's the case the whole thing is too far-fetched for any jury to swallow. This life-long grudge thing for instance. Carpenter is going to deny it. He'll tell them that he loves you like a brother. That he invited you here for the sabbatical of a lifetime. He'll apologize for his vanishing trick which he'll put down to pressure which the jury will accept because everyone accepts the notion of pressure these days – it's the universal, catch-all excuse for every crime in the book. You'll be made to look like an insensitive, self-important foreigner who's piqued because his old friend went AWOL while experiencing acute woman trouble. A Tasmanian jury will love that. It'll be all male. Even if we were to get a woman or two they'd be hillbilly rednecks who will think Lorraine was a brazen hussy and deserved all she got.'

'All right,' said Tudor. 'So what are you going to do?'

'As little as possible,' said Sanders. 'I'll take statements from everyone. I'll submit a confidential report to our Director of Prosecutions, who is a close friend. We'll discuss it. We'll put the file away.'

'You'll close it?'

'I didn't say that exactly. It'll stay half open at least. Your friend Carpenter will know that.'

'That's not very satisfactory.'

'No,' said Sanders. 'A lot that happens in my job is far from satisfactory. Knowing someone is a criminal and not being able to get a court to agree is a bugger sometimes. This being a case in point. I'm sorry.'

Ashley drove him to the airport.

Tudor didn't want this but Ashley insisted and Tudor suddenly felt too drained and limp to argue.

His premature departure was publicly explained by a crisis

back home at the University of Wessex. In a sense he was sad to go. He disliked failure and he had been looking forward to Tasmania.

'Pity you're leaving so soon,' said Ashley, as they drove out of suburban Hobart and up through dusty hills of pine and eucalyptus. 'I was looking forward to taking you on a long bushwalk.'

'That's hardly the most tactful remark,' said Tudor.' A long bushwalk was how this wretched business started.' The man was unbelievable, he thought, watching him change gear and lane as if he hadn't a care in the world.

Dame Edith had been sorry to see him go. So sorry, in fact, that over a glass of Rymills (not sparkling for once) she had said wistfully that she didn't suppose Tudor would ever contemplate the headship of St Petroc's? Tudor contemplated the title of Master of St Petroc's College, Hobart, Tasmania with almost as much wistfulness, but knew perfectly well that the time for such daydreams was long past. If it had ever existed. At least he had been able to scupper Ashley's own aspirations in that direction. He had delivered a vicious, confidential hatchet job on his former friend and the Dame had listened with a lack of surprise which was in itself disturbing.

'They say that owners take on the characteristics of their dogs,' she remarked. 'But few of us realize that dons assume the personality of their special subjects. Ashley's is violent crime. Mine is what most people, erroneously, call hedgehogs. Rather me than Ashley, don't you think?'

The job would probably go to Jazz Trethewey who also expressed regret at his departure.

'Bloody hell!' she had said. 'And we'd hardly been amused by each other's presumption.'

'Oh I wouldn't say that,' said Tudor.

'Wine joke,' she said.

Brad Davey said a tongue-tied good-bye which seemed a

compound of embarrassment and relief.

Tasman Penhaligon didn't say goodbye at all.

Sammy was effusive and obsequious though unconvincing.

'Terrible bush fires last summer.' Ashley nodded out of the window towards the stark white spars of timber stripped of all greenery and growth by the flames.

'Brad pointed them out when we drove in,' said Tudor. That had been barely a week earlier. It seemed like an eternity.

'Shall you be at the Cincinatti Crimathon?' asked Ashley.

It was as if nothing had happened, thought Tudor. Nothing at all. Ashley was behaving as if it were still pre-history; as if the last few days had never been; as if no one had been killed; no one betrayed.

'I don't know,' said Tudor. 'It may be difficult to get away. Most of the travel budget's been used on this trip.'

'Sorry about that,' said Ashley, smiling a minor thin-lipped triumph to set aside his other recent trophies.

They passed a couple of articulated trucks piled high with logs from the Tasmanian forests, a couple of taxis, a white stretched Cadillac and two military jeeps.

'You know you could still stand trial,' said Tudor.

'Theoretically,' replied Ashley, eyes on the road. 'But it's not likely. Not now.'

'So you reckon you've got away with it?'

'Looks like it.'

Tudor peered out at the hills. The sun was low and bright. He squinted at the glare.

'What did you mean about Miranda?'

'What I said.' Ashley changed down for an uphill gradient. 'Not that I'm particularly interested in technicalities. Maybe you didn't actually do it. But she preferred you. Snotty bitch.'

'Why didn't you say something at the time?'

'Don't be childish. You know what they say about revenge.

Best eaten cold.'

The airport signs said five kilometres to go. Tudor couldn't wait.

'Perhaps I shall be your Moriarty,' said Ashley.

'I'm not with you.'

'The Napoleon of crime. Unsinkable. An arch-enemy. An adversary too powerful.And never too far away. Liable to crop up any moment at crime conferences around the world ready to test and torment.'

'That makes me Sherlock Holmes,' said Tudor, 'and I hardly think—'

'Oh come, come,' said Ashley, mocking.

'Actually to be honest, Ashley, I don't care if I never see you again.'

'Dear boy,' said Ashley, shook his head and lapsed into silence until they arrived at Hobart International, one of the world's great little airports, not much more than a windsock and a couple of portacabins.

He parked under a No Parking sign immediately in front of the main departure gate. Tudor remembered that when Brad met him just a few days earlier he had parked immediately under the No Parking sign at arrivals. There was obviously something in the local genes – a distaste for authority, he supposed. The cases were easily unloaded. He had arrived travelling light and, as usual, had acquired little or no moss. He realized, with an unexpected stab of regret, that Basil the dog was the one new acquaintance he would really miss.

'Don't come in,' said Tudor. He was afraid they were going to have to shake hands. He didn't want to but that crippling English dislike of unpleasantness and confrontation made him accept Ashley's proffered palm of peace.

'No hard feelings, old boy,' said Ashley.

Tudor couldn't bring himself to say anything articulate but grunted in as non-committal a manner as possible.

'Well,' said Ashley, releasing his hand, 'Life's full of surprises. I'm sorry you have to leave. Maybe we'll get together in Cincinatti. Have a good flight meanwhile. You deserve a rest.'

He laughed not altogether pleasantly. 'Back to peace and quiet eh?' he said, waving farewell. 'No more surprises for a while.'

'Goodbye,' said Tudor, wishing he could have thought of something cutting. On the other hand 'goodbye' had a crisp finality to it. There was no going back on goodbye. Curtain. End. Finis. Part of his life brought to an end with a jolt. But at least and at last, Thank God, it was finally over.

He walked through check-in, security and passport control in a daze of relief. He took off his shoes, emptied his pockets, confirmed that he'd packed his bags on his own, had never been a member of the Communist Party, had never been convicted of a crime – hollow laughter – shut his eyes in the departure lounge, walked out across the tarmac when the flight was called, shuffled up the steps in to the aircraft, flopped down in his window seat, fastened his seat belt, sighed with gratitude for a release from stress and shut his eyes again.

He dozed and was comatose through take-off only opening his eyes as the aircraft banked past the craggy Wurlitzer, turned left over Hobart City and headed out across the ocean in the direction of home.

'Thank God for that!' he murmured, as he looked down on the Tasmanian coast and the seat-belt sign went off.

'Well, hi!' said a familiar voice. The seat next to him was empty, but the aisle seat was occupied. The words came from there. 'What a coincidence,' said his fellow passenger.

He turned and saw the pouting, dangerous smile and the shrewd, scheming eyes of little Miss Burney.

'Actually not a coincidence,' said the girl. 'I specially asked to be put near you. I need someone to hold my hand. Never been out of Tasmania before and now I get to go all the way to Great Britain. Real exciting.'

'Huh?' said Tudor.

'Didn't Professor Carpenter explain? The college has these travelling scholarships. And I've been awarded one. Well, between you and me, the scholarship committee's very small. I'm not even sure there's anyone else on it apart from the Professor. And just guess what else he's fixed up for me?'

The girl felt in a bag and produced a letter on official St Petroc's paper which she handed to him.

She smiled gleefully. It was from Professor Ashley Carpenter, Department of Criminology, University of Tasmania and it was addressed to The Vice Chancellor, University of Wessex, Casterbridge, Wessex, UK.

It was short, brutally so.

Dear Vice Chancellor,
Further to our telephone conversation, this is to introduce Elizabeth Burney, one of my most talented and interesting students. She is much looking forward to spending at least one semester with you at Wessex and studying for modules which will contribute to her final degree here at Tasmania. I'm sure you will find her a stimulating presence. As discussed, Dr Cornwall and I will liaise over the details of her tuition.

The girl giggled softly.

'I guess Ashley forgot to tell you. Surprise, surprise!'

Readers are invited to visit
the author's Web-site at
www.timheald.com or
www.timheald.co.uk